THE TOMB OF HEAVEN

FATHOM'S FIVE BOOK FOUR

ROBIN KNIGHT

The Tomb of Heaven © 2017 Robin Knight
Self-published in the USA Robin Knight 2017

All rights reserved. No part of this book may be reproduced or transmitted in any form or by any means, electronic or mechanical, including photocopying, recording, or by any information storage and retrieval system, without permission in writing from the publisher.

This book is a work of fiction. Names, characters, places, situations and incidents are the product of the author's imagination or are used fictitiously. Any resemblance to actual events, locales, or persons, living or dead, is purely coincidental.

This book is licensed to the purchaser only. Duplication or distribution via any means is illegal and a violation of International Copyright Law, subject to criminal prosecution and upon conviction, fines and/or imprisonment. This eBook cannot be legally loaned or given to others. No part of this eBook can be shared or reproduced without the express permission of the publisher.

Published by Robin Knight

BOOKS BY ROBIN KNIGHT

SERIES

MULLIGAN'S MILL

The Invention of Wings: Mulligan's Mill Book One

The Secret Love of Bea: A Mulligan's Mill Short Story

The Blooming of Bud: Mulligan's Mill Book Two

The Bend in River: Mulligan's Mill Book Three

MY BILLIONAIRE

The Billionaire's Boyfriend: My Billionaire Book One

The Billionaire's Wedding: My Billionaire Book Two

The Billionaire's Wish: My Billionaire Book Three

FATHOM'S FIVE

The Cross of Sins: Fathom's Five Book One

The Pyramid of Puzzles: Fathom's Five Book Two

The Dame of Notre Dame: A Fathom's Five Short Adventure

The Eye of Doom: Fathom's Five Book Three

The Tomb of Heaven: Fathom's Five Book Four

The Temple of Time: Fathom's Five Book Five

The Tears of the Golden Tiger: Fathom's Five Book Six

The Thief of Thunder: Fathom's Five Book Seven

The Dark Prince of Poisons: A Fathom's Five Short Adventure

STANDALONE NOVELS

ROMANTIC-COMEDIES

The Chocolate Works

The Fake Prince Jake

ROMANCE

A Boy Called Rainbow

Heartless

One in a Million

The Pathfinders

The Pearl

Under the Arabian Sky

ADVENTURE

Drive Shaft

Scott Sapphire and the Emerald Orchid

MYSTERIES

The Lost Boy

THRILLERS

Harm's Way

Into the Jaws of Wolves

To the End of the Line

STANDALONE SHORT STORIES AND NOVELLAS

A Cousin to Kiss

Anchor of My Heart

And the Beagle Makes Three

Be My Valentine, Bobby Bryson

Behind Our Eyes

Chained To You

Claiming Casey

Hotel Pens

Santa's Big Secret

The Boy from Brighton

The Cat's Pajamas

The Declaration of Love

The Nutcracker

The Salt on my Skin

The Stepbrother on his Doorstep

Untangling Tristan

Video Store Valentine

SHORT STORY SERIES

CONFESSIONS OF A STRAIGHT GUY

Bro Job

Ripped

Stripped

Study Buddy

Touchdown

For all the adventure-lovers!
Thanks for taking this rollercoaster ride with me.

THE TOMB OF HEAVEN

FATHOM'S FIVE BOOK FOUR

ROBIN KNIGHT

1
THE ISLAND OF SAINT-AVENTIN, MAURITIUS

THE HELICOPTER CIRCLED the sky high over the aqua waters of the Indian Ocean before descending toward the helipad located atop the research station.

The facility was a large hexagonal cement block connected by a long pier to a small, postcard-perfect island. This was Saint-Aventin, an island less than half a mile in diameter, inhabited only by those who worked at the private research station that had been built there. Scientists, maintenance staff, and even a Michelin-star chef made up the tiny population, all employed by Dr. Maurice Moreau, the exorbitantly wealthy owner of the facility.

Shane spotted the research station first. Sitting in the back of the chopper being flown by Moreau's pilot, he gestured with a nod of his head for Jake to look out the window as the chopper pitched left and began its descent.

"Why do I get a bad feeling about this?" Jake asked in a voice low even for Shane to hear but not the pilot.

"Why do you ask?" Shane replied in his Texan accent, one eyebrow raised in mock suspicion. "Is it because Dr. Moreau's lab looks kinda like a villain's lair from an old spy movie?"

"In a word, yes," Jake nodded. "Are you sure this is such a good idea?"

"Relax, would ya? Everything's going to be fine. Dr. Moreau is one of the leading geneticists on the planet. He's also a fanatic when it comes to ancient apothecary. You put his profession and his hobby together, and he's the one person in the world who knows the truth behind the Tomb of Heaven."

"I've still got a bad feeling. We should have brought Luca and Will along, just as back-up."

"We're simply here to ask a few questions. And if I remember correctly, you were the one who put your hand up first for this trip. You said you needed the distraction."

"I do," Jake said, looking away in frustration. "I feel useless sitting there watching over Eden, just waiting for him to get better. I want him back."

"He's gonna be okay," Shane said, reaching out and squeezing Jake's shoulder reassuringly. "Eden's gonna be back on his feet in no time, I promise."

It wasn't until they had returned from China that Shane and the others began to truly notice the moments between Jake and Eden. All of them were concerned for Eden after his fall at the Zhang Diamond Tower in San Francisco, but Jake had taken it particularly hard. On the long journey back to the island of San Sebastian he had held Eden's hand, stroked his brow, and talked to him even when he wasn't conscious as though he believed his words could be heard.

But Eden's recovery was slower than anyone anticipated, and Jake had been a lone wolf too long to withstand the feeling of helplessness any longer.

The moment Professor Fathom told them of the incident surrounding the Keys to Rasputin's Riddles, Jake knew it was his chance to get away and do something—anything—to keep his mind off Eden's rehabilitation.

Now, however, as they descended toward the bunker-like

research facility below, Jake was questioning whether this was the kind of distraction he needed.

"Relax," said Shane, feeling the tension in Jake's shoulder. "Before you know it we'll be back on San Sebastian and Eden will be feeling as good as new. All we have to do is meet with Dr. Moreau, find out who might have stolen the Keys to Rasputin's Riddles, then we'll be on our way back home."

"You sound so eager to enter the secret laboratory of Dr. Doom down there," Jake said with more than a hint of sarcasm.

"I'm sure the good doctor doesn't appreciate being called names. Besides, he's probably a lovely old man..."

"...with a scar down one side of his face and a purring cat on his lap," Jake tacked on.

As the chopper settled on the helipad, Shane and Jake both looked with trepidation at the enormous Polynesian man in a tuxedo, awaiting their arrival.

Jake shot a glance at Shane. "Let me guess, this guy's straight out of Henchmen School."

Shane grimaced in agreement. "By the looks of it he graduated top of his class."

The Polynesian man opened the door to the chopper and gestured for the two visitors to disembark. "Gentlemen," he said loudly over the whir of the helicopter blades. "Welcome to Saint-Aventin. Doctor Moreau is expecting you in the Aquatorium. Please, follow me."

Jake and Shane walked briskly behind the large-framed man who led them to a set of stairs descending into the hexagonal structure.

Leaving daylight behind, Jake and Shane followed their guide inside the facility and along a series of metal walkways that weaved through a kaleidoscope of blues and greens dancing on the surface of two enormous water tanks on either side of the men. There were no handrails on the walkways, and with more than just a little trepidation both Shane and Jake noticed a large, ominous fin gliding through the waters.

"Is that what I think it is?" Jake asked nervously as the fin followed menacingly alongside them.

"You might like to watch your step," was the only response given by the Polynesian.

Jake couldn't take his eyes off the fin… and the colossal dark shape to which it was attached, moving slowly through the blue waters. Shane was looking in the opposite direction at the two other huge fins moving silently through the water a short distance away.

"Are you still sure this is such a good idea?" Jake asked Shane again in a low voice.

"Remain alert, not alarmed," Shane whispered back. "And whatever you do, don't trip."

When they reached the end of the walkway and left the tanks behind, Jake and Shane both let out an audible sigh of relief.

"Dr. Moreau is this way," said the large Polynesian as he began to disappear down a metal spiral staircase leading to a lower level.

Jake and Shane followed him deeper into the facility.

This time, they descended into a circular, light-filled room lined with plush blue curtains and decorated with enormous coral sculptures of all colors. Chandeliers like ornate, crystal jellyfish hung from the ceiling. Several tables adorned with candles and flowers made it feel more like a restaurant than a room in a research lab. Interspersed throughout the table were tall cylindrical glass cabinets, each filled with what looked like the relics of ancient laboratories: centuries-old chemistry sets and measuring beacons; leather-bound books dedicated to body parts and poisons; barnacle-covered medicine bottles from old shipwrecks.

At a table in the middle of the empty restaurant sat a small man in a white suit with a rather large cranium. He wore a pair of thick, white-rimmed glasses and a white bowtie to match, and had been sipping soup from a bowl until the moment his guests arrived.

After quickly patting his lips with a cloth napkin, he rose to greet them.

"Ah, gentlemen. Welcome to Saint-Aventin. I see you've met Jupiter." The man in the white suit gestured to the large Polynesian man. "My name is Dr. Maurice Moreau."

"I'm Shane Houston. And this is Jake Stone."

"I know who you are. The reputation of Professor Fathom and his men precedes you all. Don't take that as a compliment, you have a tendency for meddling in things you shouldn't and a certain knack for creating chaos wherever you go. I can't imagine how high your insurance premiums are. Needless to say, I would appreciate a little care and respect while you're here. This room we're standing in is my haven, my sanctuary from the world. This... is my Aquatorium. The world's only underwater 5-star restaurant set inside a research facility."

With a clap of the doctor's hands, the blue curtains lining the room slid open to reveal a large glass wall—which was all the separated them from the tanks they had passed above... not to mention the three Great White sharks now circling the room, intently watching the humans inside the glass restaurant.

"Gentlemen, you're just in time for lunch," Dr. Moreau informed his guests.

"Please tell me we're not on the menu," Shane said with a nervous laugh.

The doctor laughed in response... then simply said, "Won't you join me at my table?"

Dr. Moreau led the men to his table, where Jupiter pulled out a chair each for Jake and Shane then took a seat beside them.

"I trust you don't mind if Jupiter joins us," Dr. Moreau said. "Just for security reasons, you understand. One can never let one's guard down."

With that, Jupiter opened his suit jacket, pulled a pistol from his shoulder holster and placed it on the table, leaving his hand resting on it.

The largest of the three sharks glided by the floor-to-ceiling glass separating the men from the water tanks.

Shane glanced from the shark to Dr. Moreau. "Haven't you heard the saying, people in glass restaurants shouldn't shoot bullets?"

"If there's any need for Jupiter to fire his weapon, he won't be aiming at the glass," Dr. Moreau said with a polite smile. "No offence."

"None taken," Jake smiled back. "But please be assured, we're not here to cause any trouble. We just have a few questions."

"Yes, you're here to ask about the Tomb of Heaven. Herr Schroeder informed me that Professor Fathom wants to know if the legend is true, which begs me to ask the question... why?"

A cautious look passed between Jake and Shane.

Dr. Moreau noticed, then smiled as though a realization had just dawned on him. "Someone has stolen the Keys to Rasputin's Riddles."

"Is that a question or a statement?" Jake asked.

"Take your pick. It was only a matter of time before someone's curiosity got the better of them. But are they wasting their time trying to find the Tomb of Heaven?"

"That's what we're here to ask you," said Shane.

Dr. Moreau raised one eyebrow. "Isn't that something we'd all like to know. What precisely is inside the Tomb of Heaven? If the historians and scientists are correct, then the tomb will be nothing more than an empty chamber, if it even exists at all. But if the writings and ramblings of the mad monk's disciples are correct, then the tomb could hold the answer to immortality itself. The elixir of life. The concoction that made the monk Rasputin almost superhuman, enabling him to miraculously survive one assassination attempt after another so that he could flee to his unknown hiding place. A place they call the Tomb of Heaven."

For a moment, the doctor watched the sharks circling the restaurant, his mind pondering the enormity of the conversation. "Do you know why it's called the Tomb of Heaven?"

Jake and Shane shook their heads.

"Because if the elixir of life does exist... if Rasputin created a potion that would grant eternal life... if he actually managed to bottle immortality... then there's no need for heaven anymore."

"Does it exist?" Jake asked matter-of-factly.

"If you're asking me if I stole the Keys to Rasputin's Riddles, the answer is no. I prefer to search for immortality via more scientific methods. For me the answer is right here." With a wave of his hand, he gestured to the three giants ominously swimming around them, watching them.

"These creatures are not simply my life's work. They are my world. My children. They are the epitome of perfection—nature's grand design, created more the 420 million years ago and still they rule supreme over seventy percent of our planet. Unlike humans, their actions are not clouded by emotions. They are driven purely by need. They're not susceptible to desire, greed, ego or even cancer. They're smart, powerful, feared and respected. Some would argue that's the very definition of God, which is why my work on the anti-angiogenic properties in the cartilage of a shark's skeleton will change the world forever. In my view, these creatures are the closest thing to immortality on this earth."

"So you don't believe the tomb exists," said Shane.

"I didn't say that. I said there are faster ways of finding the secret of eternal life. Tracking down the Tomb of Heaven is an intricate and problematic quest. First you need to uncover the location of the tomb, something that nobody has ever been able to pinpoint despite countless theories and attempts. Secondly, you need to be in possession of the Keys to Rasputin's Riddles which have until recently been part of the private collection of reclusive New York billionaire Edgar Davenport... but now seem to have been, shall we say, liberated by an unknown yet motivated party. Last but not least, you need to solve the riddle on each of the five crypt doors leading into the tomb. After that, you'll either be rewarded with the elixir of life... or certain death."

"Certain death?"

"A place filled with trials and traps can't be good for your health," Dr. Moreau remarked.

"Says the guy with a bunch of sharks swimming past the window," muttered Jake.

Shane kicked him under the table and shifted the conversation back to the topic at hand. "Word has it a faction from the North Korean government is behind the theft of the Keys to Rasputin's Riddles."

"If you're asking me to confirm or deny rumors, I'll do neither," said Dr. Moreau.

At that moment, someone began to descend the spiral staircase. Without even seeing his face, the uniform and napkin draped over one arm suggested the man was a waiter.

"Ah, lunch is served," said Dr. Moreau.

Silver chopsticks and four plates were placed on the table, one each in front of Jake, Shane, Dr. Moreau and Jupiter. Shane and Jake did not look at the waiter, but rather down at the meal before them. Petite slices of raw fish decorated with orange and black caviar and garnished with luminous green seaweed petals sent waves of suspicion across Jake's face.

"There's nothing 'fishy' about this fish, is there?" he asked.

Dr. Moreau laughed. "Mr. Stone, have you never tried sashimi? The tuna and kingfish are a favorite in Japan."

Jake and Shane both picked up their chopsticks and, after a brief pause, began eating.

Jupiter devoured several slivers of raw fish.

The Tomb of Heaven

Meanwhile, Dr. Moreau held a slice of fish to his lips. But instead of eating it, he added, "Of course, when it comes to sashimi, the fugu fish isn't quite as popular as tuna and kingfish, namely because... well... it's fatal."

Dr. Moreau started laughing.

Jake and Shane instantly stopped eating.

"Fatal?" Shane uttered, spitting out the fish in his mouth.

"As I said before," Dr. Moreau chuckled. "You have a tendency for meddling in things you shouldn't."

"You've poisoned us all?" Jake breathed.

"Not all of us. The waiter was instructed to serve Jupiter and I a much more edible portion of sashimi. The two of you, however, were served fugu. You see, I know exactly who stole the Keys to Rasputin's Riddles. It's the same person who just made a sizeable donation to my research facility to help fund my work... and to make sure the two of you never make it out of here alive."

Both Dr. Moreau and Jupiter began laughing even louder.

With a sharp clang, a silver chopstick suddenly fell onto a plate.

But it wasn't Shane's or Jake's chopstick.

It belonged to Jupiter who, with a guttural, choking sound, stopped laughing and began to clutch at his throat with both hands.

"Unfortunately," interrupted the waiter, speaking in a crisp British accent, "your usual kitchen staff are tied up in the kitchen... literally. Sorry to say, old chap, but I may have gotten the meals switched around the wrong way."

With a stunned look on his face, Dr. Moreau glanced from Jupiter to the waiter, as did Jake and Shane who both gasped. "Daniel?"

Dressed as Dr. Moreau's waiter in a white shirt and black tie, British reporter Daniel West winked from behind his black-rimmed glasses and shot a quick smile at Shane. "Miss me?"

That's when Dr. Moreau dropped his chopsticks—

9

—and reached for Jupiter's gun on the table.

Jake instantly threw himself across the table to get to the weapon first, but Moreau was closer. His spindly fingers wrapped themselves around the gun and he raised it quickly, aiming it straight at Jake.

Jake swiftly rolled left off the table.

Moreau pulled the trigger.

The bullet missed Jake by an inch.

It ricocheted off the metal spiral staircase a short distance away and came back at them.

Shane grabbed Daniel and crashed to the floor just as the stray bullet clipped the cuff of Daniel's flailing arm.

Then everyone watched, almost in slow motion, as the bullet hit the glass wall.

A tiny jet of water sprayed into the room.

Dr. Moreau stared, wide-eyed and horrified.

Jupiter stopped choking and managed to gasp.

Jake looked up and simply whispered, "That's not good."

Shane and Daniel jumped to their feet to see cracks like lightning streaks spread ominously across the glass.

As though they knew what was about to happen, the three Great Whites outside the wall swiftly gathered, almost grinning at the promise of—

CRAAAAAAAACK!

With an ear-splitting smash the glass wall shattered into smithereens, followed by the roar of rushing water as what was outside the restaurant suddenly came in—

—including the monstrous shapes of three Great White sharks as they were swept into the restaurant.

"Oh fuck!" uttered Shane as he grabbed Daniel's hand and raced in the opposite direction of the oncoming wave. "Get to the stairs! Get to the—"

The flood of water knocked him and Daniel clean off their feet.

The Tomb of Heaven

Jake looked up to see an eighteen-foot shark being swept toward him, side-on, like a truck that had jackknifed on a freeway. Seconds before it could slam straight into him, Jake leapt onto the table at which they had been sitting. The wave of water crashed into the table and sent it flying. Jake jumped again, this time grabbing hold of one of the crystal jellyfish chandeliers.

The Great White sailed by underneath him, flapping and floundering furiously. There was not enough water in the restaurant for the shark to take control of the situation... at least not yet.

But as the torrent continued to flow in from the tanks outside, the Aquatorium flooded fast.

Hanging from the chandelier, Jake looked below him to see Dr. Moreau clamber onto a tabletop just as the table was picked up by the rush of water and transformed into a floating raft.

He saw Shane and Daniel do the same a short distance away, gasping for air as they pulled themselves out of the water and scrambled onto an unsteady table just as the second Great White was swept into the flooded room, swirling around them, it's enormous body gaining balance and momentum as the water level rapidly rose.

Jupiter—still clutching his swelling, choking throat—was not as swift climbing to safety as the tables began to lift off the floor and swivel and topple around the room.

He tried to clamber onto one of the tabletops, his arms grabbing frantically, but all he managed to do was flip the table over with his weight. He tried to scream for help but his throat was so swollen from the poison that no sound could get out... and no air could get in.

Jupiter floundered in the water, his tongue bulging in his mouth as his throat closed around his windpipe.

He body began to convulse.

His arms flapped and splashed in the water.

His eyes looked up in terror, drenched in salt water and the grim realization that he only had moments left to live.

But it wasn't the choking poison that killed him.

With an almighty thrashing of its tail fin and a gnashing of giant jaws, one of the Great Whites lunged at Jupiter and bit him in two with its razor sharp teeth, devouring the top half of the large Polynesian and leaving his legs to bob and kick in a sudden torrent of bright red.

"Oh shit," Jake said as he dangled from the chandelier. He glanced quickly to the spiral staircase twenty feet away before his eyes caught sight of the air vent next to the chandelier. Hurriedly he began climbing his way to top of the jellyfish-shaped light fixture.

That's when the chandelier began to give way under his weight.

The wiring quickly threaded its way out through the ceiling socket.

The whole chandelier dropped several inches before coming to a jolting stop.

Jake held his breath, realizing at any moment the chandelier could plunge into the shark-infested water with him still clinging to it.

Slowly, placing one fist over the other, he began climbing as cautiously as he could up the chandelier towards the air vent.

Down below, a huge fin cut the red water, circling the tabletop upon which Shane and Daniel tried desperately to keep their balance.

The shark turned sharply and rammed into their table.

Daniel lost his footing and almost slid into the water before Shane grabbed his arm and pulled him so close that Daniel's body pressed hard against him, his arms wrapping themselves around the Texan.

"How do you always manage to do this?" Daniel uttered frantically, his eyes filled with alarm.

The Tomb of Heaven

"Do what?"

"Get yourself into the most ridiculously life-threatening situations."

Shane shrugged, not taking his eyes off the shark that was about to turn and ram them once more. "It's a gift, I guess. Hold on!"

The shark crashed into the tabletop once more and Shane and Daniel held on tight, their feet slipping on the table while they managed to keep their balance… for now.

Across the room, Dr. Moreau was crouching on a tabletop of his own, paddling with both hands to try to reach the spiral staircase. He panted in short, panicked breaths. Sweat raced down his huge cranium while his glasses fogged up. He stopped paddling for one brief moment to wipe the mist from his spectacles, just in time to see the giant head of a shark emerge from the water directly in front of him.

Dr. Moreau gasped and scrambled backwards, slipping off the table top—

—and straight into the open jaws of a second shark that emerged from the water behind him.

"My children!" the doctor squealed, just as the Great White clamped its jaws shut.

Blood jetted out the sides of its mouth and Dr. Moreau's severed limbs fell into the water.

"Shane! Daniel! Get out of the water!" shouted Jake from above.

Shane and Daniel both looked up to see Jake clinging to the chandelier, but as he called to them, the chandelier dropped another few inches from the ceiling.

Shane saw another chandelier hanging almost directly above the tabletop on which he and Daniel teetered. "You have to get to that chandelier," he told Daniel in no uncertain terms.

"What about you?"

"There's no time to argue with me, Daniel." Two fins cut

through the eater and circled the bobbing table. "I'll give you a leg up, hurry."

Daniel did as he was told and put his foot in Shane's clasped hands. With a quick hoist, Shane boosted Daniel up to the chandelier.

Daniel grabbed hold of the light as tight as he could with one hand and reached down with the other. "Shane, come on!"

Shane shook his head. "It won't hold us both."

As if to confirm his point, the chandelier dropped six inches from the ceiling socket.

Jake's chandelier did the same a moment later.

"I'm not leaving you," Daniel said.

But the decision whether Shane stayed on the table top or jumped for Daniel's hand was not theirs to make.

With an almighty crunch, one of the Great Whites snapped its teeth down into the side of the tabletop on which Shane stood, taking the table in its jaws.

The tabletop tipped upward.

Shane lost his balance.

He fell on his ass on the wet surface of the table then slid down toward the shark, only stopping when his feet hit the shark's nose.

Infuriated and still biting down on the table, the shark pushed its way through the water, its tail fin propelling them away from the staircase.

Dangling helplessly from the chandelier, Daniel shouted, "Shane!"

The chandelier dropped several more inches.

"Daniel, listen to me." The voice came from Jake. "You have to swing. Swing from the chandelier and make a jump for the staircase. You can do it."

Daniel looked in one direction to see Jake. Then in the other direction to see the staircase only ten or so feet away.

On the far side of the room, the shark had bitten off a chunk of Shane's tabletop and was chewing it into splinters while Shane tried desperately to regain his balance.

"We have to help Shane," Daniel said.

"We can't do it from up here," Jake replied urgently. "You need to swing to the staircase, then I can swing to your chandelier and do the same. But we gotta hurry."

The wiring dropped another three inches and sparks showered down from the socket above Jake.

Below them, another Great White began to swim in a figure eight, waiting for them to fall.

Daniel began to move his weight back and forth, the chandelier jingling as it swung like a pendulum while Daniel took aim at the staircase.

At the same time, Jake began to swing on his chandelier, ready to make the leap for Daniel's chandelier the moment Daniel made the jump for the stairs.

Across the room, two sharks circling Shane's table began to tussle in the water, the tension rising over which one was going to claim Shane as their next meal. Bullishly they barreled and bumped each other, the frenzied flicks of their tails knocking into Shane's mauled table and sending him dropping to his knees on the table top, once again struggling to keep his balance.

As Daniel and Jake swung like acrobats in unison, the shark below them showed more and more confidence, lifting its head out of the water and opening its jaws in anticipation of a kill.

Daniel and Jake swung wider and wider.

Jake's chandelier dropped another few inches.

So did Daniel's.

There was no time left.

"Jump!" Jake shouted, at the same time releasing his own chandelier.

As Daniel let go of the light fixture and sailed through the air towards the spiral staircase, Jake made the leap for Daniel's swinging chandelier.

Below him, the shark snapped at Jake's feet, missing him by an inch as he flew from one chandelier to the next.

Jake grabbed onto the swinging crystal light fixture.

Daniel slammed into the handrail of the spiral staircase, almost losing his grip and slipping back into the water. But his fingers clutched the iron banister with all his might.

Quickly he pulled himself over the handrail and onto the steps.

He looked to see Jake swinging.

The chandelier was dropping.

Sparks flew as the wiring broke completely.

Jake used the last of his momentum and threw himself at the spiral staircase.

Daniel reached out for him, grabbing him by the shirt as Jake fell short.

Jake's flailing arms managed to hook the handrail but his legs missed their footing and slipped into the water.

With all his strength, Daniel hauled Jake up onto the banister.

Jake lifted his legs quickly out of the water just as the shark lunged, chomping on an iron step as a consolation prize and twisting the metal in its jaws.

Gasping for air, Jake pulled himself over the handrail to safety. "Thanks," he panted.

But Daniel was already looking back toward Shane. "We have to save him! What can we do?"

Jake watched as the shark with the twisted metal step in its mouth turned away from the staircase to join the other two Great Whites menacing Shane. "Do you know how to act like a clown?"

"What the hell are you talking about?"

"Ain't you ever been to a rodeo? The clowns are always there to rescue the cowboy at the last second."

Jake climbed over the handrail and stood on the outside of the staircase, holding on tight to the banister. Daniel did the same. "But we're not at a rodeo," he said.

"We're about to be," Jake replied.

With a loud whistle, Jake got Shane's attention. "Hey Tex! Do you wanna be shark bait or do you wanna get your ass the hell outta here right now?"

Shane rolled his eyes. "What the fuck do you think?"

"Then pick your bull and open the gates, cowboy!"

Shane looked from Jake to the sharks and back again, realizing exactly what Jake was suggesting. "Are you out of your mind?"

Jake shrugged.

One of the sharks took another chunk out of the table.

Jake may well have been out of his mind, but Shane was out of both time and options.

"Ah shit," he muttered to himself.

Then, with a deep breath, Shane threw himself onto the back of the nearest Great White shark as it circled his splintered table.

Instantly the beast began to thrash.

Its tail slashed back and forth through the foaming water.

Shane grabbed onto the gigantic dorsal fin in front of him and dug his heels into the side of the Great White with all his might.

The shark bucked and arched and churned up a tempest.

The other two sharks were triggered by the frenzy and began nosing and shoving the Great White that Shane was riding, sensing its distress and zeroing in for an attack.

That's when the shark launched itself through the water, powering away from the other two predators and heading straight for the spiral staircase.

It veered left, it turned right.

Shane tried to steer it by pulling on the dorsal fin.

He saw Jake and Daniel ahead, leaning from the banister of the staircase, ready to grab him.

From either side, the other two Great Whites began to charge and attack, butting into the body of the shark Shane was riding, their teeth tearing at its flesh.

The Great White under Shane swam even faster, heading

straight towards the spiral staircase at full speed until—

Smash!

With a crash that almost knocked Jake and Daniel off the structure, the shark hammered into the spiral staircase, its nose twisting the base of the stairs into a mangled, metal mess.

At the top of the structure, bolts flew out of the ceiling and the spiral stairs groaned, threatening to collapse with the impact of the mighty shark.

Jake and Daniel held on for dear life.

They reached down and grabbed Shane, already trying to clamber off the shark and onto the staircase.

With another jolt the other two sharks slammed into the stairs.

The structure shifted loose from the framework attached to the ceiling.

"Go!" Shane shouted as Jake and Daniel pulled him over the handrail and onto the stairs. "Go, go, go!"

Daniel, Jake and Shane charged up the stairs, circling their way toward the exit and leaping from the structure just as the spiral staircase broke loose and collapsed into the flooded Aquatorium below.

Metal hit the water with a great splash as the sharks thrashed about furiously, searching for human flesh before turning on one another.

Shane watched the gruesome scene of crimson-frothed chaos before saying to Jake and Daniel, "Let's get the hell outta here."

"Where to next?" Daniel asked, wiping his wet hair out of his eyes.

"We're going to New York to see Edgar Davenport and find out exactly how much he knows," Shane answered, before adding sternly, "And you, my handsome reporter, are heading straight back to England."

"You're not getting rid of me that easily," Daniel smiled. "I get the distinct feeling this adventure is only just beginning."

2

NEW YORK CITY

BEFORE THE RESCUE OPERATORS, shark handlers and local authorities from Mauritius could fully contain the incident at the Moreau Research Facility, Jake, Shane and Daniel managed to slip through the mayhem and were evacuated from the Island of Saint-Aventin along with Moreau's shocked and bewildered lab employees and maintenance staff.

Twenty-four hours later, they were standing on the tree-lined terrace of Edgar Davenport's Park Avenue penthouse overlooking the Manhattan skyline. The city lights began to shimmer and twinkle like a ball gown as the dusk sent bright pink and orange trails blazing across the sky.

"My apologies for keeping you," said a voice as the pair of French doors leading out to the terrace opened.

Jake, Shane and Daniel turned at once to see a distinguished gentleman in a smoking jacket step out and close the French doors behind him.

"It's a beautiful view, don't you think?" said the man. "It's pretty much the only view I ever see. I don't get out much these days." By way of introduction he extended his hand. "I'm Edgar Davenport, by the way."

Jake was the first to shake his hand. "Yes, we know. I'm Jake Stone, this is Shane Houston and Daniel West. Thank you for seeing us."

"Thank you for showing an interest in my situation," Davenport replied. "When Herr Schroder explained that you wanted to see me, I was delighted."

"You know of us?"

"Everyone in the world of antiquities and artifacts knows of Professor Fathom and his men. Your reputation—"

"—precedes us, so we've heard," said Jake.

"Then you know about the Keys to Rasputin's Riddles?" Davenport asked.

Jake nodded.

Davenport let out a worried sigh. "The theft of the artifact is under investigation by the police, the F.B.I. and the C.I.A., but to be perfectly honest, I'm not entirely convinced anyone truly appreciates the potential gravity of this situation. When they're not busy bickering over jurisdiction, they're questioning the legitimacy of the artifact altogether. I heard the head of investigations describe it as 'hocus pocus'."

"Do you believe that the Tomb of Heaven contains some sort of... elixir of life?" asked Shane.

"To be honest, I'm not sure what I believe. I'm a collector, Mr. Houston. An investor in ancient curiosities. I trade mystical treasures much the same way some people trade shares—it's a business. But I always believed the Keys to Rasputin's Riddles was something... special. Now it appears the North Koreans want to use it to get their hands on whatever's inside that tomb."

"With all due respect, Mr. Davenport, we don't know who stole the Keys yet, or why," Jake pointed out.

"With all due respect, Mr. Stone, I think the reason is more than clear. Somebody wants to unlock the mystery to eternal life."

"From what we understand, they have their work cut out for

them if that's their intention," said Daniel. "The Keys to Rasputin's Riddles is only one part of the puzzle, correct?"

Davenport nodded. "Yes, that's correct. But where there's a will there's a way, Mr. West. When I was seven years old I worked as a shoeshine boy on Wall Street. Today, I practically *own* Wall Street. If someone wants to find the Tomb of Heaven badly enough, they'll find it. And God help us all when they do. Which is why I always had a contingency plan in place."

He turned to Jake, Shane and Daniel and said, "Gentlemen, will you join me in my library for a moment? There's something you need to know."

If Edgar Davenport's library was any indication of his style and taste, then this was a man who preferred things minimalist, refined and to the point.

Maps and prints hung on pristine white walls, perfectly framed and sealed behind glass. White shelves were built into the walls, lined with books of exactly the same height. Artifacts and relics were housed inside glass casings, each labeled with a small, engraved, gold plaque. The room was organized to the point of perfection.

In the center of the library was a long desk made entirely of white marble. On it was a single lamp, its halogen globe pointing down to a manila folder sitting on the desk's surface.

Davenport escorted his guests to the desk and opened the folder. He handed Jake an enlarged photograph.

"Gentlemen, this is a picture of the Keys to Rasputin's Riddles which was on display here in New York at the Davenport Trust Building. This is what's been stolen."

Jake, Shane and Daniel looked at the photo. To say they were a tad surprised at what they saw was an understatement.

"*These* are the Keys to Rasputin's Riddles?" asked Jake.

"They're *matryoshka* dolls," said Daniel. "You're telling us that the keys are a set of *matryoshka* dolls?"

"Indeed they are," replied Davenport. "Or more commonly known as Babushka or Russian dolls. A doll within a doll within a doll, and so on. Are you familiar with Russian culture, Mr. West?"

"I worked as a foreign correspondent in Vorkuta for two years. Every home you go to has a set of these on the mantle."

"They come in all different colors and costumes, depending on the region," explained Davenport. "The number of dolls in each set also varies greatly. The Keys to Rasputin's Riddles has five dolls in all. Legend has it they were handcrafted by Rasputin's disciples, each one a key to one of the five crypt doors leading to the tomb."

"How does one of these dolls work as a key?" asked Shane.

Davenport opened the folder on the desk and spread several ink-smeared, hand-drawn diagrams in front of them, each sealed in a protective, plastic sleeve.

"These parchments are rumored to be the unfinished blueprints of the crypt doors. From the drawings, it appears the doors were intended to be carved from stone. The mechanics of each door is different, but when the correct doll is placed here, in this small alcove, the door will open."

"What if the wrong doll is placed in the alcove?" asked Jake.

"Then these triggers on either side of the alcove will activate a stone vice that will slam shut on the doll, pulverizing the key instantly, sealing the alcove."

"If there's only one key for each door, that would mean the door would remain locked," said Shane.

"Forever," Davenport nodded.

"So whoever tries to open the crypts doors, gets one shot and that's it," said Jake. "But how do you know which doll opens which door?"

Davenport pointed to a stone slab at the top of each door. "In this slab is written a riddle. The riddles haven't been included in these diagrams, only on the doors themselves. The answer to each riddle is in some way painted on each doll. A color. A symbol. An expression on the doll's face. Who knows what the answer is without knowing the riddle first."

Jake looked again at the photograph of the five dolls.

The largest doll depicted a maiden wearing a dark blue headscarf and an intricately painted dress with multiple shades of blue, green and white. In one hand she carried a lantern.

The second painted doll had a headscarf of crimson red and a matching dress. In her hands was cradled a white skull with black empty sockets for eyes.

The third doll had a yellow headscarf with a bright orange dress. Her feet were bare, and in her hands she carried a tiny pair of shoes.

The fourth doll had a white headscarf with a purple shawl. On one arm was a basket in which she carried a knife, a hammer and a scroll of parchment.

Finally, the fifth and smallest painted doll had a headscarf and dress as black as midnight. On her headscarf were ribbons tied into bows, while in one hand she carried a ball of string and in the other a single key.

"You're right," Jake said. "There's no telling what any of these clues mean without first knowing the riddle. But how does the mechanic in the door know which doll is the correct doll?"

"Since the beginning of time, volume and mass have been used to trigger locks," Davenport said. "The Ancient Egyptians used the weight of an object as a mechanic in many of their secret chambers, as did the Aztecs and the Mayans. If my guess is correct, there's a weighing plate at the base of each alcove. If the doll with the incorrect weight is placed in the alcove, the vice will destroy the doll and keep the door sealed shut for all time."

"So if the person who has stolen the Keys to Rasputin's Riddles gets one answer wrong, the Tomb of Heaven will remain sealed forever," Jake said.

"They won't just get one answer wrong," said Davenport. "They'll get them *all* wrong."

Jake, Shane and Daniel looked away from the diagrams to see Davenport step away from the desk, his hands clasped behind his back.

Davenport took a deep breath, then crossed the room to a drinks trolley and took the lid off a crystal carafe filled with whisky. "Drink anyone?"

"Hell, why not?" said Jake. "I think we may need it."

Davenport poured four tumblers of whisky, neat, and handed one each to Jake, Shane and Daniel before sipping his own. Then with a deep breath he said, "There's one vital piece of information you need to know. The keys that were stolen are fake. Whoever broke into the Davenport Trust Building took a forgery. A decoy."

"What do you mean, a decoy?" asked Jake. "Why?"

"As a warning bell. If someone is determined enough to steal the artifact, then they're determined enough to find the Tomb of Heaven. Unfortunately, if they try to use the fake keys to get inside, they'll destroy the locks and seal the crypt doors forever. That leaves us no choice but to find the tomb before that happens."

"Us?" asked Daniel, his eyes lighting up as he glanced at Shane.

Davenport nodded. "Time is of the essence... and I need your help."

Shane spoke up first. "Mr. Davenport, we appreciate your faith in us, but if you already have the C.I.A working on this case, don't you think—"

"Mr. Houston, this incident has been met with nothing but red tape and skepticism from the start. While the authorities fight over jurisdiction and joke about the seriousness of this case, there's someone out there on the brink of finding what may well be the most important discovery in the history of humankind. If

The Tomb of Heaven

it does indeed exist, the elixir of life will change the world forever. It cannot fall into the wrong hands. I need you to find the Tomb of Heaven before someone else does."

Shane looked from Davenport to Jake.

A moment of silence passed between them before Jake asked, "If the artifact in your collection was a fake, where are the original keys?"

"Hidden in plain view on a shelf in a market stall in Karachi, Pakistan," Davenport answered matter-of-factly. "The owner of the stall, Mr. Ahmed Zahid, is an old acquaintance. He was my guide on an expedition to a ruined temple at the foot of the Himalayas many years ago. Now he sells trinkets and souvenirs. The only thing he'll never sell is the set of Russian dolls collecting dust in a far corner of his stall. Of course, he has no idea just how valuable they are. All he knows is that the dolls pay for his children's education. That's all he *wants* to know."

Davenport put his tumbler of whisky down on the desk. "Gentlemen, I want you to go to Karachi and get the keys. Then I want you to find the Tomb of Heaven. I'm willing to pay you... quite handsomely."

"We don't do this sort of thing for money," said Shane.

"So I've heard. You do it to try and make the world a better place. You do it to right wrongs and balance the scales. You do it to keep the demons away." Davenport picked up his tumbler of whisky then drained the remainder of the glass. "Can you imagine a demon more dangerous than one who can live forever?"

At that moment, the door to Davenport's library opened and a young butler appeared.

"Sir, if you'll pardon the interruption, there's a telephone call for you," said the butler.

"Thank you, Salinger," Davenport said, before turning to his guests. "Gentlemen, please excuse me. My time is rather precious and I must leave. Salinger will show you to the door. In the meantime..." He pulled a pad and pen from a drawer in his desk, scribbled a few words and tore off a piece of paper to hand to Jake. "This is where you'll find Ahmed. I hope you find much more."

Jake pocketed the piece of paper before he, Shane and Daniel put down their glasses and followed Salinger from the room, leaving Davenport in his library.

The butler led them through the penthouse apartment to the front door, where Daniel and Shane left the palatial residence.

At the last moment, Jake glanced down and noticed the scuffs on Salinger's black shoes. He winked and patted the young butler on the shoulder. "I know a great shoeshine kid down on the Eastside who could always use a new customer and a tip. You never know, he could become the next Edgar Davenport."

Salinger glanced down at his shoes then politely smiled. "I'll tend to it immediately. Thank you, sir."

With that, Jake left the apartment and Salinger closed the door behind him.

Out on the street, car horns blared and pedestrians pushed by on the hurried way home from work.

"So what now?" asked Shane to Jake.

"We catch the first plane to Karachi in the morning," he answered simply.

"You don't think this guy might be a little... eccentric? I come from Texas money. I *know* eccentric. Have you met my mother, Gertie? Hell, this guy's talking about the elixir of life! The lost fate of the Russian Empire! Rasputin, the mad monk himself, who's been dead for over a hundred years!"

"That's a front page story if ever I've heard one," piped up Daniel. "Even if it's not true, it'll have the print presses running hot all over the globe. I can see the headlines now—"

Shane promptly pressed his palm against Daniel's chest. "You're not coming. No way, no how!"

Daniel stared at him, shocked. "Why the bloody hell not?"

"Because it's too dangerous."

"I lived in Russia for a year. I know its people, its culture."

"All you want is a story."

"All you want is an adrenalin rush."

"You'll get yourself killed following us."

"You'll get yourself carjacked before you even leave the airport parking lot in Saint Petersburg. Shane, I speak Russian. I solve puzzles. I can decipher the riddles. What are you not getting here?"

"You! I'm not getting you. This is exactly what happened last time. We solved the Riddle of the Sands and you flew home to England for your story."

Daniel blinked in shock. "Are you making this about you and me?"

"No, you are," answered Shane. "You're the one who just turned up out of nowhere."

"And saved your lives!" Daniel added.

"And thank you for that. But right now you need to get back on a plane to London and—"

"Shane, zip it!" interrupted Jake. "Daniel's right, we need him. And right now, you two lovebirds need to get a room somewhere and get some shut-eye. We leave for Pakistan first thing in the morning. I'll see you at the airport."

With that, Jake started to walk away.

"And where the hell are you going?" Shane asked, pissed at Jake's bossiness and his sudden departure.

"I live here, remember? At least I did in another lifetime. I want my own bed. I'm going home for the night."

With that, Jake turned quickly and headed off into the busy Manhattan night, swiftly vanishing in the crowd of bustling New Yorkers, leaving Shane and Daniel to their own devices.

"We'll take two rooms for the night, thanks," Shane told the desk clerk at the hotel, just as someone started a screaming match on the second floor while the drunk asleep on the frayed sofa in the lobby began snoring.

The desk clerk—a fat, bald man in an undershirt that had once been white—glanced from Shane to Daniel with a quizzical look.

"You know this ain't the type of hotel where two people book separate rooms, right?"

"It's the only place we could find at short notice," Shane replied, annoyed.

"It's just that normally we cater for hookers and their clients who just want a good time," the clerk pressed.

"That's not what we're here for," Shane assured him.

"That's a shame," said the clerk, eyeing Shane up and down. "You could make a pretty penny in this town what with that Texan accent and those broad—"

"I'm not a hooker," Shane declared.

The clerk shifted his gaze to Daniel and his lips curled at the edges. "So Clark Kent here is on the hustle, huh? I like the look. Nerdy yet sturdy. Do you keep the glasses and tie on when you—"

"He's not a prostitute either," Shane said. "We just need two rooms for the night and that's it."

"Suit yourself," the clerk said with a disappointed shrug before turning to a board behind him covered in numbered hooks. A grin crossed his face once more. "Well, well, whaddaya know. We've only got the one room left anyway. What can I say, it's tight-ass Tuesday."

He plucked the last remaining key off the board and Shane took it from him. "Fine, we'll take it."

"That'll be fifty bucks. Plus another fifty deposit in case you break anything. Like the bed," he added with a wink.

Shane slapped two fifties onto the desk.

"It's on the first floor, second door on your left. Don't do anything I wouldn't do," grinned the desk clerk.

But Shane was already on his way to the stairs with Daniel in tow.

Inside their room, the pair stood grim-faced as they looked upon the torn wallpaper, the rickety old double bed and a splintered dresser with a bowl on top filled with complimentary condoms and pillows of lube.

Through the wall on either side of the room they could hear the sex of strangers in stereo, the moaning and groaning from other hotel guests bouncing back and forth from wall to wall.

Daniel was focused on other things. "Is that a bloodstain on the carpet?"

"I think so," answered Shane flatly.

"Couldn't they get a rug to cover that?"

"I don't think they could find one big enough."

Shane stepped around the dried lake of a bloodstain. "You can have the bed, I'll sleep on the floor… somewhere."

"Oh bloody hell, Shane. What on earth is wrong with you?"

"Nothing," Shane answered curtly.

"That's bullshit. Ever since we left Mauritius you've had your defenses up."

"Maybe you shouldn't have been in Mauritius in the first place. Why were you there anyway? You nearly got yourself killed. What were you looking for, another mystery to solve? Another front-page scoop? Another chance with me? Sorry to break it to you, Daniel. You may have got your headline last time, but you missed out on getting your man."

"Are you accusing *me* of being the one who walked out on our relationship?"

"We didn't have a relationship."

"We had *something*."

"And *you* gave it up for your job."

"Me? You're the one who had to go gallivanting around the world on another bloody adventure. Have you ever tried keeping up with you, Shane Houston? Have you ever tried tracking you down? It's not bloody easy."

"Then how *did* you track us down in Mauritius?"

Daniel paused a moment. "Someone contacted me."

"Who?" Shane started pacing the room angrily. "Did you get a tip-off from some sleazy underworld snitch? Was it one of your money-grabbing secret sources trying to sell a story? Who told you what we were doing at Dr. Moreau's lab? Who?"

Daniel took a breath. "It was your professor."

Shane stopped in his tracks. "Professor Fathom?"

"He said you could use my help. He said there may be trouble."

"What did you say?"

Daniel looked Shane in the eye. "I said I'd do anything to keep you safe."

For a moment they stood, caught in one another's gaze.

Then with sheer, unbridled lust in his eyes, Shane cut a beeline straight over the bloodstained floor to Daniel.

His arms wrapped themselves around Daniel's waist at the same moment his lips planted themselves on Daniel's.

The moan that escaped them both was instantly muffled by their locked mouths, while their tongues delved deep inside, exploring the warmth they had both missed so much.

Shane squeezed Daniel's dark hair, his fumbling fingers knocking Daniel's glasses off-center.

Daniel didn't care, he wasn't looking through his glasses anymore anyway. His eyes were shut, his mouth open, and his hands went in search of the buttons to Shane's shirt.

He unsnapped them hastily, breaking the top button off altogether before unfastening the rest and pulling the tucked shirt out of Shane's jeans. He pulled it off the large, muscled balls of

Shane's shoulders and opened his eyes to drink in the sight of the Texan's magnificent torso.

Daniel smiled.

As Shane watched his shirt sail to the floor, he pushed his hips hard up against Daniel's, their bulging crotches pressing against one another. He forced Daniel backward until Daniel's back thumped into the old dresser.

Daniel grunted as the knobs of the dresser drawers jabbed him in the back.

The dresser rocked, then banged against the wall as Shane shoved Daniel hard up against the dilapidated piece of furniture.

Shane quickly unbuckled his belt and began unzipping his jeans, all the while keeping the weight of his body pressed hard against Daniel, pinning him to the dresser.

At the same time, Daniel started wrestling with his tie until Shane shook his head and told him, "No, leave it on. Leave your shirt and tie on, the glasses too. I think that clerk was onto something... Clark Kent."

Daniel grinned. The thought of turning Shane on was a turn-on in itself.

With his heart thundering in his chest and his hands floundering with his belt, Daniel managed to get his trousers undone at the same time that Shane slid his own jeans down over the firm round cheeks of his ass.

Simultaneously the two men pushed their pants down their thighs, unleashing their stiff, thick cocks at the same time.

At once, the two shafts of manhood slapped against each other, slipping and sliding over the silky, veined skin of their shafts until Shane and Daniel began grinding their hips together, grunting and yearning for more as they crushed their cocks between their stomachs.

Daniel let out a series of groans as Shane began pushing against him in a slow rhythm, the dresser thumping against the wall with each powerful heave of his body.

Daniel reached down between them and took a firm of both their dicks in one fist, laying Shane's shaft on top of his and squeezing as tight as he could.

Shane let out a loud moan and a breathy, "Oh fuck." He bit his bottom lip and began shoving his groin into Daniel harder and faster, sliding his cock back and forth in Daniel's grip.

The banging of the dresser turned into a tribal drumbeat.

Not to be outdone, the couple on the other side of the wall began groaning even louder, their bed head banging against the wall in time with the dresser.

Daniel felt a hot drizzle of precum ooze over his shaft from the eye of Shane's cock.

It was followed by Shane biting desperately on Daniel's earlobe as he mumbled, "I want to fuck you. I want to come inside you—right now."

Daniel's response was swift and decisive.

Releasing their cocks from his grip, he spun around, his trousers still around his knees. He was now facing the dresser, his ass beckoning for Shane's dick.

Hastily Shane reached over him, fumbling for a condom and lube from the bowl.

He bit open the condom wrapper and slid it over his cock with urgent expertise, then popped the pillow of lube and smeared the cool gel down Daniel's ass crack, fingering his hot, soft hole with two moist fingers.

Daniel gasped and took a firm hold of the dresser, ready for what was to come. "Fuck me," he panted, his glasses fogging up. "Do it now."

Shane didn't need to be told twice.

Swiftly he removed his fingers from Daniel's ass, and taking his large hard cock in one fist, he guided himself inside Daniel's passage.

Daniel filled his lungs to capacity, taking in an enormous

breath of air as Shane slowly slid his dick all the way inside his British lover.

Once Shane had filled him completely, Daniel released the air from his chest before Shane gently pulled himself almost all the way out of Daniel.

Before withdrawing completely, he pushed his way inside Daniel once more, faster this.

Daniel groaned.

"Harder," he uttered. "Fuck me harder."

Shane took hold of Daniel's left hip with one hand, while he reached over Daniel's shoulder with his right hand and took hold on the black necktie, wrapping it around his fist before bringing it back over Daniel's shoulder and pulling on it as though he had Daniel by the reins.

Daniel groaned even louder.

Shane thrust himself into that hot, lubed ass again and again.

Harder now.

Harder and faster.

The dresser bashed against the wall.

Daniel tried to steady himself against the rickety piece of furniture with one hand while his other hand clutched at the necktie to prevent it from choking him.

"Am I hurting you?" Shane asked.

"I like it," Daniel panted, pulling on the tie as though they were in a tug-of-war. "Don't stop. I want you to come inside me. Come inside now."

Shane started pounding Daniel's ass even harder.

The dresser hammered against the wall.

Thump-thump-thump-thump.

Daniel grunted loudly with each forceful thrust until—

Suddenly a leg of the dresser gave way and snapped off.

The dresser dropped three inches, then lurched forward.

As it began to topple, Shane grabbed Daniel around the waist and quickly shuffled them both backward toward the bed.

They staggered away just as the dresser tumbled forward and smashed against the floor.

With their feet caught up in their trousers and Shane's cock still inside Daniel, the pair teetered for a moment before falling onto the bed.

Daniel grunted through clenched teeth as Shane's cock seemed to ram itself even deeper inside him the moment they landed on the bed. But there was no stopping their act of lovemaking. Sweating and steaming up his glasses, Daniel now straddled Shane with his back to him.

Desperately he began to ride the Texan, pumping up and down on Shane's cock while Shane continued to pull on the necktie.

"I'm coming," Shane soon panted. "I think I'm gonna—"

Before he could finish his sentence, a jet of cum gushed from the eye of his cock, surging into the head of the condom.

Daniel felt the instant heat of Shane's orgasm and without even touching his own shaft, his throbbing, bobbing cock launched one, two, three loads of cum into the air and across the room.

"Fuck!" he cried out, shutting his eyes tight. "Oh fuck! Yes!"

Shane gritted his teeth and squinted as he thrust his hips upward, pushing another three or four wads of cum into the condom, filling it to the brim.

"Oh God," he breathed. "Oh fuck, that was good."

Gasping for air he threw his arms out wide and tossed his head back onto the bed.

Daniel winced as he released one last ooze of cum, before gently sliding himself up Shane's still hard shaft and letting out of sigh of relief.

"Holy shit," he panted as he collapsed on the bed beside Shane.

He pulled off his fogged-up glasses just in time to see Shane lean in for a kiss.

Their lips danced against each other, tenderly kissing before Shane propped himself up on one elbow and gestured to the smashed dresser. "Well, I don't think I'll be getting my fifty dollar deposit back."

Daniel propped himself up beside Shane. "I hope a night with me is worth more than fifty bucks."

"Sure is," Shane grinned. "I'd pay at least seventy-five."

Daniel laughed. "I guess that makes me a real catch."

Shane kissed him once more. "Yes you are."

Jake unlocked the door to his warehouse apartment and pushed it open to the sound of mail sliding across the floor. Several dozen letters and bills had been shoved under his door in his absence. He bent to pick them up now, and closed the door behind him before wandering into his empty home.

It felt abandoned and long forgotten.

It felt as though he had never really lived here at all.

Since meeting Professor Fathom, he could count on one hand the number of hours he'd spent in this apartment. He wondered if it would ever become his home again, or if his place in this world now belonged on San Sebastian with the professor and Sam... and Eden.

Jake sat himself down in a chair, resting his unopened mail in his lap while he set his watch alarm for five in the morning so he could get to the airport on time. He let out a deep sigh, then closed his eyes for a minute.

From outside he could hear the commotion and bustle of the city he loved so much. A siren wailed by. Someone whistled for a cab. A garbage trunk clanged and roared in the alley behind the warehouse. It was a city of strangers, a city in which anyone could easily become lost, which is how Jake had always lived his life.

Lost and content.

Until now.

Perhaps he was finally ready to be found.

Perhaps the real Jake Stone was tired of being a stranger, and was ready to be loved.

That's when he heard the shower water in the bathroom begin to run.

Jake sat up with a start and turned to look at the curtain that partitioned the bathroom from the rest of the apartment. Steam rose from behind the curtain.

"Who's there?" Jake demanded.

Nobody answered.

The water continued to run.

Visions of finding Sam passed out in that shower, poisoned by Pierre Perron, flooded Jake's mind and sent him into a panic. Jake had never felt so helpless in his life as he did the day he opened the shower curtain and saw the young homeless boy unconscious in the tub, barely breathing, barely alive. Sam meant more to Jake than Jake had ever admitted to the kid. He wondered if he would ever tell Sam about their true relationship.

But now as he stood from his chair, Jake knew that it couldn't be Sam who had turned the shower on. Sam was back at the plantation house on San Sebastian with the Professor and the others. He had vowed to leave New York forever and find a new home, there was no reason he would ever return.

"Who's there?" Jake demanded again.

Again there was no response.

Slowly Jake began making his way across the old hardwood floors of the warehouse apartment. He prepared himself for the possible outcomes to the scenario. Perhaps an old pipe had burst. Perhaps a squatter had moved into the apartment in his absence. Or perhaps one of his many enemies from the past was trying to get his attention by luring him into a trap.

As Jake stepped up to the bathroom curtain, the only thing he was sure of was that he was about to find out the answer.

He took a firm hold of the curtain.

He flung it open.

And there, standing naked under the running water of the shower, he saw—

"Eden?"

As the steam rose, Eden turned. Water raced in tiny rivulets down his toned, tanned body. Streams ran down his handsome face as he opened his eyes, saw Jake and smiled.

"I didn't hear you come in," was all Eden said.

Jake stared at him, confused but thrilled. "What are you doing here? You're supposed to be back on the island. You're supposed to be in bed. You were barely conscious when I left."

"I'm better now," Eden said. "I'm better now that I'm here. With you."

Jake felt a tug at his heart and a twinge in his crotch. He glanced from Eden's smile to his glistening cock and watched it quickly harden.

"Come here," Eden said from under the warm flow of water.

Jake did as he was told.

He stepped up to Eden as the Brazilian's shimmering cock rose, its shaft long and straight, its head emerging from beneath the sheath of veined skin.

Jake swallowed, his heart hammering in his chest, before Eden reached out with one wet hand and took him by the shirt, pulling him into the shower.

Willingly, Jake stepped over the edge of the tub and under the running water, fully dressed, boots and all. He didn't care.

He let the shower flow over his hair, his face, his shirt, his jeans.

He let the cascade drench his clothes and soak through to his core.

And as Eden leaned forward, he let the beautiful Brazilian lay his lips on Jake's lips, kissing him tenderly. Passionately. Longingly.

Eden touched Jake's jaw gently with his fingers, and for a brief moment he pulled out of their kiss and whispered, "Wherever you are, that's where I want to be. Just stop running, Jake. Please stop running."

"I will," answered Jake without hesitation. "For you, I'll do anything."

As Eden's lips began kissing a trail down Jake's jaw, his chin, his throat, Jake gazed upward, watching the steam rise through the air.

It floated above the curtain.

It drifted through the rafters.

It danced about the fire sprinklers.

And suddenly—

—a fire alarm rang loud and startling.

Jake sat bolt upright in his chair, sending the unopened mail falling from his lap and scattering across the floor.

Quickly he realized that the sound that woke him was not the fire alarm, but his watch alarm.

Quickly he realized the shower was not running—

—and that Eden's presence was nothing but a dream.

A beautiful, heartbreaking dream that cried out to be real.

The washed-out light of another New York dawn was spilling through the windows.

"Fuck," whispered Jake, pushing himself out of his chair.

He headed for the door.

He left the mail on the floor.

And Jake abandoned his apartment once more.

3

KARACHI, PAKISTAN

THE NOISE ROSE from the city like the dust from the frantic streets and the smells from the ramshackle food stalls on every garbage-lined corner. Car horns blasted relentlessly, bus brakes hissed and squealed, live poultry squawked and flapped in wooden cages stacked beside market stalls, whistles pierced the air as police officers tried to divert the morning traffic through an intersection of malfunctioning traffic lights, and thousands of people bustling up and down the street shouted their conversations to one another trying to be heard over the cacophony of chaos that was Karachi.

"According to the map, just down there is the entrance to the Old Bazaar," said Shane, pointing beyond the whistle-blowing police officers. It was a small side street lined with bamboo scaffolding and paper lanterns hanging on wires that crisscrossed from streetlight to streetlight.

"Where's the hotel?" Jake asked.

Shane pointed ahead of them. "Just up here. The Royal Jasmine."

Jake, Daniel and Shane all looked to the opposite corner to see a four-story hotel that had clearly seen better days. Chunks of the building's façade had fallen away, and the steps leading up to the wide, open-air entrance of the hotel were decrepit and crumbling.

As the three men made their way across the street and up the steps to the open-air lobby, they saw that the interior of the hotel was as much in need of repair as the outside. The dated wall hangings were frayed, the chandelier dangling above a fountain in the lobby was missing several crystals and light bulbs, while the fountain itself—with a chubby Cupid at its center—was completely dried up, its statuesque grandeur covered in dust and its tiles chipped and cracked.

But what the hotel lacked in appearance, the desk clerk made up for with enthusiasm.

"Gentlemen, gentlemen, welcome to the Royal Jasmine Hotel, the pearl of Karachi," said the old Pakistani man with the thick twirled moustache behind the front desk. "My name is Saahir, your most humble host. Are you intending to stay at our luxury resort and enjoy all the many benefits it has to offer, including its close proximity to the Old Bazaar, individual climate control in every room with the exception of the second and third floor, as well as our complimentary Ceylon tea delivered to your room each and every night, not to mention our very popular rooftop pool which, according to our Kazakhstan Tripadvisor guests, is a five-star feature of our most finest establishment?"

"Does the pool have more water in it than the fountain?" asked Jake, not intending to make a joke.

The man behind the desk laughed heartily. "You are American. I can tell not only by your accent but your sense of humor. Very witty. Very, very witty! I trust you will tell all your friends about your visit to the Royal Jasmine Hotel, which offers clean sheets on every bed and breathtaking views over Karachi from the windows in rooms 204 and 205 which, unfortunately, are under renovation at the moment."

"What are the views from the other rooms?" asked Daniel dubiously.

"A most picturesque historical brick wall erected in 2009 to house the telemarketing company next door," Saahir said with the smile of a salesman. "For your convenience we also have an elevator that operates Mondays, Thursdays and Saturdays," he added, gesturing to an old freight elevator at the far end of the lobby with doors wide enough to fit a car. "Fortunately for you, today is Thursday. Although if you're in a hurry may I recommend taking the stairs anyway. It's a lot faster."

"Thanks for the advice," said Jake. "Now can we please book a room for the night?"

"Most certainly, sir" Saahir said excitedly. "One room with a view of the picturesque historical brick wall coming right up."

A throng of merchants, shoppers, tourists and traders milled through the labyrinthine lanes and passageways of the Old Bazaar, shouting and haggling over rolls of silk fabric, tins of tobacco and spices of every color imaginable. Everything was on sale at the Old Bazaar, from exotic birds to snapping crabs, from tailored suits to leopard-print luggage.

As Jake, Shane and Daniel made their way through the entrance of the bazaar, Daniel paused a moment and hooked the strap of Jake's backpack with one hand to halt his stride.

"What's the matter?" Jake asked.

Daniel gestured to a ladder leaning against the rickety bamboo scaffolding that covered the entire entrance of the bazaar. The scaffolding creaked under the weight of the dozen or so men applying a fresh coat of paint to the old façade.

"You're about to walk under a ladder," Daniel said. "Do you know how unlucky that is?"

Jake chuckled. "Hell, we parted ways with luck a long time ago. We've been flying by the seat of our pants ever since."

Casually he walked under the ladder into the bazaar, followed by Shane who grabbed Daniel's hand. "Now remember what I told you. Try not to get yourself killed."

"I'll do my best, but thanks for the tip."

Shane led Daniel under the ladder as they followed Jake through the entrance into the noisy, colorful, chaotic markets. Instantly they were grabbed and pulled by merchants wanting their business, desperately trying to sell them everything from cheap cigarettes to fake brand-name colognes, from leather shoes to live snakes.

Jake and Shane just ignored the commotion, while Daniel apologized profusely for rejecting every eager salesman who tried to bargain with him.

"According to Davenport, Ahmed Zahid's stall is in the south corner of the bazaar," said Shane.

"How do you know where we're going?" asked Daniel. "This place is a maze."

"Maps are my thing, remember?"

At that moment, Shane turned left, glanced down a narrow lane in the bazaar and said, "That looks like it to me. Come on."

The three men headed for a modest little market stall crowded with shelves covered in ornaments of all description. Silver lamps, gemstone necklaces, wood-carved chess sets and bejeweled shishars lined every inch of every shelf. And in amongst this cramped little treasure-trove was a modest-looking man dusting each piece of merchandise with care and dedication.

When he saw the three men enter, he smiled as if to greet new customers, before realizing exactly who these strangers were.

"You've come for the *matryoshka*, haven't you." It was a statement, not a question, and it was one filled with hope instead of dread.

"Yes," Jake replied. "Are you Ahmed Zahid?"

The man nodded emphatically. "I am he."

"Davenport sent us. Do you have the doll?"

"Yes, yes, of course." The man started laughing with relief.

The Tomb of Heaven

"I'll be so glad to see it returned to Edgar. I've hidden it for years now, but a secret can only remain that way for so long."

Hurriedly the man scampered off to a dimly lit corner of his stall before returning with the Russian doll.

Jake, Shane and Daniel instantly recognized it as the largest doll from the pictures Davenport had shown them, the one depicting the maiden with a blue, green and white dress and a lantern in one hand.

"I don't want to know what it is or what it's worth," said Ahmed. "My children will soon finish school, I have no need for it anymore. Please, just take it from me. The sooner it is gone, the easier I will breathe."

He thrust the doll toward Jake, pushing it into his chest with so much urgency that Jake had no choice but to take the doll.

Cautiously Jake opened the first doll to make certain all the other dolls were inside, then he swiftly slid it into his backpack like a tourist who had just purchased a trinket for his niece back home.

"Do not take offence," Ahmed said, picking up the keys to his stall and gesturing for the three men to leave. "But please go. Go now. I beg of you."

As Jake, Shane and Daniel were shuffled out into the market lane, Ahmed swung the iron-grated door of his stall shut and locked himself inside. Without another moment's hesitation he placed as *Closed* sign in the window and turned out the lights.

Jake, Shane and Daniel simply looked at each other for a moment before Daniel asked, "Did we say something to offend him?"

"I guess he's just not the kinda guy who likes company," Shane answered with a shrug.

"Speaking of company," Jake added, tightening the straps on his backpack. "I think we may have some of our own."

Shane and Daniel instantly followed Jake's gaze to the far end of the market lane to see two figures wearing brown robes, their faces concealed beneath hoods. Their presence was immediately ominous. Instinctively Shane glanced in the opposite direction and saw a third hooded figure at the other end of the lane.

People were already sidestepping and scurrying away from the robed men, sensing danger.

"I think this is our cue to leave," said Shane. He nodded to a passage of stalls veering off to the left. "Follow me, gentlemen."

Hurrying through the crowd, Shane, Daniel and Jake scurried down the passageway, their movement setting the hooded figures into motion as they swiftly pursued them, pushing past shoppers and merchants who shouted in anger and shrieked with surprise.

The commotion set off a wave of panic in the crowded bazaar.

People began to push and shove one another, frantically stepping out of the way of the hooded men who began charging at full speed through the bazaar in pursuit of Jake, Shane and Daniel.

One of the assailants kicked over baskets filled with beads, sending innocent tourists and shoppers tripping and slipping to the ground.

Another of the hooded men pulled a knife and cut the ropes holding up a display of rugs, sending carpets flipping, flopping and unfurling across the narrow alleyway of the bazaar.

From the opposite direction, the third assailant pulled over a long fish tank containing dozens of snapping crayfish and crabs, smashing the tank to smithereens and sending the crustaceans spilling and splashing across the cobblestoned ground.

More people screamed and scattered as chaos followed in their wake.

The three hooded men made a sharp turn, heading up the narrow lane into which Jake, Shane and Daniel had disappeared.

Up ahead, Daniel glanced over his shoulder. "Who the hell are those guys?"

"I don't know, but let's not hang around to find out," answered Shane.

They raced past a white-bearded clockmaker with cuckoo

clocks chirping. They ran past a tailor proudly buttoning a suit jacket onto a mannequin. They sprinted by a vendor selling lanterns made from polished brass and stained glass, hanging a string of lights in front of his stall.

Seconds later, the hooded men bolted by, smashing over several cuckoo clocks, their cogs and gears wheeling across the lane. They kicked over the neatly dressed mannequin in the suit and cracked open its smiling face. They snapped the string of lanterns and sent the ornate lights crashing and shattering to the ground.

Daniel glanced back again. "Bloody hell, they seem mean."

"Eyes on the getaway," Jake reminded him, yanking Daniel to the left before he crashed into an unsuspecting tourist. "Shane, which way outta this maze?"

Still running, Shane quickly sized up their position, his mind counting up the number of labyrinthine passageways they had passed as his eyes scanned left and right. "This way," he said, pointing to a darkened passage just beyond a merchant selling an assortment of tropical parrots and live reptiles.

As they passed the stall, a bright blue bird wolf-whistled at them.

Jake looked at the parrot. "Hey, do us a favor and shit on the guys chasing us, would ya sweetheart?" he asked the bird.

The parrot winked and squawked, "You betcha, pretty boy."

The passage was so narrow that Shane had to turn his broad shoulders, scurrying sideways until he reached a steep set of concrete stairs heading upward. Daniel and Jake followed suit.

With a glimpse back over his shoulder, Jake paused and caught sight of the three hooded men rounding the bird stall just as the parrot turned its back to them, raised its tail and squirted shit all over them.

The parrot laughed then flapped its wings and headed for the safety of the rafters as one of the hooded men kicked over its perch.

"Screw you, asshole," the bird shrieked.

The hooded men continued the chase.

Jake laughed then charged up the stairs, scraping the sides of the backpack against the narrow walls.

Shane and Daniel had already vanished ahead of him.

Behind him he could hear the stomping and panting of his pursuers.

Within moments Jake burst out of the stairwell and onto a decrepit rooftop parking lot.

Dusk had set in and suddenly a pair of headlights came zooming towards Jake, accompanied by a screeching horn.

The smallest, rustiest car Jake had ever seen in his life skidded to a halt in front of him. Inside it he saw Shane squeezed behind the wheel and Daniel with his knees up around his ears in the passenger seat. They were shouting to him through the closed windows of the two-door car, as though yelling from inside a bubble. "Get in! Jump in the back!"

Jake heard the footsteps of the hooded men getting louder as they bounded up the stairs behind him.

He quickly opened the rear hatch of the clunky little vehicle. "I can't fit in there!"

"Find a way," Shane shouted.

Just then the three hooded men came racing out of the stairwell.

Jake threw himself into the tiny space in the hatch, his long legs dangling out as Shane stepped on the gas.

Before Jake could even attempt to shut the hatch, the wheels of the car squealed into motion and the rear bumper bounced with the sudden addition of Jake's weight, leaving a trail of sparks behind.

"I can't believe you stole a car!" Jake shouted at Shane.

"We didn't steal it, we're just borrowing it for a while," Shane tried to justify.

"From who? A group of clowns?"

The Tomb of Heaven

From the rear hatch, Jake saw the three hooded men watch the tiny car make its getaway.

A moment later they disappeared swiftly back down the stairwell.

"I don't think we've seen the last of them yet," Jake said as the car hit the exit ramp of the parking lot and made a speedy descent.

In the back, Jake tried to reposition himself to better take in their claustrophobic surroundings. Shane was crushed behind the wheel, one arm twisted awkwardly as he crunched through the gears. Daniel, with his knees squished against his ears, was trying to wind down his window to give himself some air—until the window winder broke off in his hand. Above them was a battered old sunroof that looked as though it had rusted shut.

"Seriously, you guys couldn't find something bigger?"

"Sorry, but all the limos were out getting detailed," said Shane with more than a hint of sarcasm. "Now will you shut up and let me drive?"

At that moment the itty-bitty getaway car bottomed out at the end of the ramp. Jake, Shane and Daniel all jolted, grunting in their cramped, contortionist positions. The open hatch swung down then up again, as did Jake's dangling legs, before the car leveled out and sped from the parking lot exit, turning onto the busy Karachi street in front of the bazaar.

The revving of motorcycle engines close behind them caught Jake's attention.

"Oh shit," he said, instantly spotting the three hooded assailants now on motorbikes.

Their headlights flared brightly, shining directly on the tiny getaway car fleeing the scene.

"Step on it, Shane," Jake said urgently.

"It's as stepped on as it gets," Shane replied with just as much urgency, blasting the screechy horn to warn pedestrians and bicycle riders to get out of the way fast.

From behind, the three motorcycles swiftly approached.

Two quickly flanked the tiny car, moving up on either side while the third motorcycle brought up the rear.

Jake hoisted his legs in the air just in time before the motorcycle plowed into the rear bumper of the car.

"Evasive action," shouted Daniel as the car jolted with the impact. "Evasive action now!"

Shane shot him a look. "Who the hell says 'evasive action'?"

"Sorry, self-confessed nerd. Too much sci-fi in my youth."

At that moment, the motorcycle on the right rammed the passenger door.

"Taking evasive action now!" Shane shouted.

He turned the wheel hard left and the motorcycle outside his window had to swerve before being hit.

Shane grinned—

—and took his eyes off the road for a second too long.

With a loud *snap!* the first bamboo-scaffolding pole cracked in half as the already dented hood of the tiny car crashed through it.

Shane gasped, realizing he'd mounted the pavement and was about to smash through a second of the bamboo poles holding the scaffolding in place along the façade of the Old Bazaar.

He jerked the wheel right to try and steer his way back onto the street, then gasped again as he almost drove straight into an old man and his cart

Shane swiftly jerked the wheel left again to avoid collision.

Snap!

A second bamboo pole shattered on the hood.

All the way down the pavement in front of them, the entire scaffolding structure began to sway and groan.

People on the street began to scream in panic as workers on the scaffolding peered over the edge.

"Shane! What the fuck are you doing?" screamed Jake.

Shane tried to veer off the pavement again, but this time the

The Tomb of Heaven

motorcycle to their right slammed into the passenger door once more, forcing the car back into the path of the scaffolding.

Crack!

Snap!

Two more bamboo poles broke.

Then an entire plank collapsed on the pavement in front of them.

Shane's knuckles turned white on the steering wheel as workers on the scaffolding jumped left and right to save themselves.

Shane turned right and left to avoid them.

"Shane!" Jake and Daniel both shouted together.

"Shut up and let me drive!"

That's when a plank came crashing down directly onto the hood of the car—

—along with four drums of paint.

In an explosion of white, the paint splashed over every inch of the windshield.

"Oh fuck," Shane whispered, no longer able to see where he was going.

He fumbled for switches and levers, desperately trying to find the wipers.

They heard another bamboo pole crack on the hood.

"Get off the pavement! Turn now!" ordered Jake.

"I can't see where I'm going!"

"Turn on the wipers!" Daniel panicked.

"I'm trying!"

Shane found the wiper lever.

He flicked it on—

—and nothing happened.

The wipers gave a feeble whir and wheeze, then did absolutely nothing.

In desperation Shane turned the wheel right, blindly veering back out onto the street.

Through the open rear hatch, Jake caught sight of the scaffolding behind them crashing to the ground in a domino effect as people leapt, paint splattered and poles broke and bounced across the street.

In the driver's seat, Shane tried to wind down his window in the hope of sticking his head out to see where his was going—

—only to have his window winder break off in his grip, just as Daniel's had.

"Fuck!"

The motorcycles on either side of them rammed into the left and right side of the car.

The motorcycle in back slammed into the bumper of the hatch, then veered swiftly to avoid the bumper as it fell off the tiny car and clanged down the street.

Hastily Jake twisted himself about in the cramped space, reached up for the rusty sunroof and punched it clean out of the roof of the car, opening a hole big enough for him to stand up and see where they were going.

The instant he emerged through the open sunroof, his eyes turned to saucers when he saw an elderly lady struggling to get out of the way in front of them.

"Left, left, left!" he shouted down at Shane.

Jake's entire frame swayed as the car veered left.

"Right, right, right!" Jake shouted again as the car careened toward a woman carrying her swaddled baby in her arms.

Shane hauled the wheel right.

"Left, left, left!" Jake bellowed louder than ever as a mother duck and her three ducklings escaped their cage and flapped into their path.

Shane jerked the wheel again.

"I think I'm gonna throw up," Daniel said, his face turning green.

"If you love me you'll swallow it!" Shane said.

Daniel gulped, a repulsed look on his face.

The Tomb of Heaven

That's when one of the motorcycles revved up alongside the passenger door.

Its rider glanced up at Jake as he stood protruding from the roof of the car.

With one hand still steering the bike, the hooded assailant lunged at Jake, snatching one of the straps of the backpack and yanking it off Jake's shoulder.

Caught unawares while trying to call directions, Jake's body twisted as the backpack was almost completely pulled off his back.

He snatched hold of the other strap just in time, pulling the hooded figure on the motorcycle into a tug-of-war for the backpack.

Jake yanked on the pack and the motorcycle wobbled precariously.

The hooded man managed to keep control of the bike with one hand and pulled hard on the pack with the other.

Jake almost lost his grip on the strap. "Get your hands off!" he warned through gritted teeth, yanking the backpack yet again, harder than before.

But the rider of the motorcycle refused to give up, the motorbike veering momentarily before he gained control of it once more.

"Jake! Some help here!" shouted Shane, still driving blind.

Jake quickly realized that Daniel and Shane had no idea of the tug of war that was playing out, unable to see through their paint-smeared windows.

"Daniel, open your door!" was all the instruction he gave.

"What?"

"Just do it. And do it hard!"

Without another question, Daniel shoved open the passenger door.

It made a loud *bang* as it slammed straight into the motorcycle beside the car, sending the rider flying off the motorbike seconds before the bike itself toppled and tumbled and skidded onto the pavement in a shower of sparks.

"Left! Now left!" Jake shouted, pulling both straps of the backpack over his shoulders and tightening them.

Shane did as Jake told him, turning sharply to avoid a man with a cart full of pig carcasses at the last second.

He straightened the wheel.

"Where to now?"

Jake heard the rev of motorcycle engines and glanced behind to see the remaining two hooded assailants still in pursuit.

He glanced ahead and saw, directly in front of them, a clear run to the stepped entrance of the Royal Jasmine Hotel.

"Put your foot on it. And hold on tight," Jake said.

Shane put his foot down hard on the accelerator and at fifty miles an hour the tiny car hit the steps leading up to the open-air lobby of the hotel.

With a *thunk, clang, grind* and *clatter* the makeshift getaway car launched itself up the steps to the lobby, catapulting into the air at the top of the stairs before thumping back down onto the tiled floor, still traveling at top speed.

"Left!" shouted Jake.

"Right!" he shouted a second later.

Shane turned the wheel and the car skidded around the fountain in the center of the lobby.

"Straight! Straight! Straight!" Jake shouted, catching sight of the open doors of the freight elevator directly ahead. He guessed, he hoped, he just knew the little car would fit inside.

They didn't really have a choice.

Behind them, the two motorcycles jettisoned themselves up the steps to the hotel and launched themselves across the lobby.

The first one managed to negotiate a sharp turn around the fountain, the back wheel chipping off a few tiles as it narrowly escaped a collision with the ornamental structure.

The second motorcycle rider, however, was not so lucky.

The Tomb of Heaven

As his front wheel hit the tiled floor, the motorcycle skidded out from under him. The motorbike crashed into the wall of the fountain, while the momentum of the impact threw the hooded rider clear over the handlebars, hurling him straight into the chubby Cupid at the center of the fountain.

With a *crack* the rider's head slammed into the Cupid, knocking the assailant unconscious and knocking the smiling little Cupid off his perch and smashing on the tiles below.

A jet of water shot into the air from Cupid's broken perch.

Jake watched over his shoulder and grinned triumphantly.

Then turned back to shout, "Brake! Brake! Brake!"

The tiny car's brakes squealed as the vehicle skidded along the lobby floor and straight into the freight elevator, its side mirrors clipping both sides of the door with a faint—*Ting!*—like a spoon being tapped against a crystal glass.

The car jolted to a halt, sitting neatly inside the elevator.

Jake looked behind them to see the last of the hooded riders speeding toward them.

He glanced around, and to his surprise he saw Saahir, their most humble host, in the elevator with them, his back pressed against one wall and a tray containing a teapot and teacups in his slightly quivering hands.

"Up," said Jake with polite urgency. "Please press the up button."

Saahir nodded. With his elbow he pressed the button for the top floor, and the doors closed just as the third hooded assailant slid to halt, thudding against the elevator doors as they shut him out.

Slowly the elevator began to ascend.

With sweat dripping down his face, Jake—still protruding from the sunroof of the car—gave Saahir an awkward smile.

Saahir gave an awkward smile back. "I see you are enjoying all the excitement that our fair city has to offer." He gestured to the tray in his hands. "I was just about to deliver our finest Ceylon tea to your room. Complimentary, of course."

"Thanks, but I think we'll give it a miss tonight," Jake said.

Saahir nodded. "Yes, of course." He noticed the paint smeared all over the car's windshield, and juggling the tray in one hand he took a napkin and said, "Please, allow me. You seem to have a little smudge on your windshield."

With an *eek-eek-eek* of the napkin, he tried in vain to wipe a little of the paint off. "Perhaps it needs a good wash."

"I think so," smiled Jake. "Say, you mentioned before that this elevator was kinda slow."

"Slow? No sir, it's not slow. It's *very* slow."

"Could someone climb the stairs faster than this elevator can reach the top?"

"Oh yes, sir. Easily, sir."

Jake thumped the roof of the car with his hand. "Shane, get ready to reverse this baby as fast as you can. We're gonna have company the second those doors open."

With a grunt and an angry whir, the car's gears were jammed into reverse.

The elevator bounced to a halt at the top floor.

Sure enough, as the doors opened, the third and final hooded assailant stood facing them. He had abandoned his motorcycle in the lobby. He had thrown his knife away. And now, with both hands, he held a handgun in his grip and aimed it straight at the car.

"Go, go, go!" Jake shouted.

The tires spun into motion.

The tiny car reversed out of the elevator.

The hooded man leapt out of the way before he had a chance to fire off a single shot.

With a somewhat astonished look on his face, Saahir watched the little vehicle reverse out of the elevator and cut a trail straight along the tiled corridor leading directly to the rooftop terrace of the hotel.

Jake turned his head then quickly covered his face with both arms as the car smashed through a pair of glass doors leading to the pool area.

"Stop! Stop! Stop!" he shouted, but it was too late.

The car crashed through a potted hedge bordering the pool area, then turned a wooden sun-lounge to splinters before the back wheels bounced over the edge of the pool and sent the car sailing in reverse—

—straight into an illuminated blue pool in the shape of a lotus flower.

The car sent a giant splash into the air and a wave over the edges of the pool.

White paint swirled through the water before bubbles erupted from the windows and hood.

Jake quickly scrambled out of the sunroof.

Both the driver's door and the passenger door opened, flooding the car as Shane and Daniel swam free.

As the little vehicle sank to the bottom of the pool, Jake, Shane and Daniel found their feet and quickly began wading to the edge.

The click of a handgun being cocked made them freeze in their tracks.

Jake, Shane and Daniel looked up to see the last of the hooded men standing at the edge of the pool, his weapon pointed straight at them.

He laughed from beneath his hood before saying in a thick Russian accent, "Long live the master."

He aimed the gun at Jake first, pointing the weapon directly at his forehead before he gently squeezed the trigger.

Crack!

The sound shattered the night air.

But it did not come from a bullet being fired.

It came from Saahir smashing his teapot over the hooded man's head so hard, the ceramic pot exploded into a million pieces.

The gun went off and the bullet missed Jake by an inch.

The hooded assailant swayed unsteadily on his feet, then his limbs went limp and his knees buckled.

He plunged into the pool, revealing a smiling Saahir who had crept up behind him.

"Nice work," Jake said, breathing a sigh of relief.

"We want your stay at the Royal Jasmine Hotel to be memorable, but not that memorable," Saahir replied. "Was he one of the vendors from the bazaar? Sometimes they get quite irate when you don't buy something."

Jake, Shane and Daniel quickly pulled themselves out of the pool, fishing the unconscious pursuer out of the water as they did so. They pulled the hood from his face to reveal a man with a thick bushy beard, pasty white skin and dark circles under his eyes.

"We have no idea who he is," Shane answered. "But he sure as hell ain't North Korean."

"No," observed Daniel. "As a matter of fact, he looks an awful lot like… Rasputin."

"Whoever he is, it's time we got the hell outta here," said Jake. "Let's dump this guy in the side alley. By the time he wakes up he won't have a clue who clunked him over the head. By the way, thanks for your help, Saahir."

Saahir beamed proudly. "A pleasure to be of service, sir."

Shane glanced from Saahir to the car in the pool, watching the bubbles blurp from the sunken vehicle. "I'm guessing an angry car owner is gonna come looking for that. Do you mind adding it to our bill? Along with any other damage we may have caused."

Saahir's smile grew even wider and his eyes lit up with delight. "As you wish, sir!

As Jake, Shane and Daniel hurriedly dragged the unconscious

hooded man away, leaving a dripping trail behind them, Saahir called after them. "I humbly thank you for choosing the Royal Jasmine Hotel, my friends. And I very much appreciate the twenty percent gratuity tip that I will be kindly adding to your account. Thank you very much in advance and safe travels. And be sure to tell all your friends about our luxurious hotel when you get home."

By the time he had finished, Jake, Shane and Daniel were gone.

Saahir smiled to himself and looked at the submerged car. A new opportunity dawned on him. "A diving wreckage at the bottom of the pool! A most unique feature. I must add it to the brochure immediately."

4

ISLAMABAD CENTRAL STATION, PAKISTAN

STEAM BILLOWED from the train and sent of veil over the travelers and station workers hurrying up and down the platform. The smell of roasted nuts from a nearby vendor filled the chill air as Jake moved past a man arguing with the train conductor over tickets while a cluster of women and girls with head scarves stood nearby, huddling together to keep warm.

The old telephone booth had a broken hinge on the door and a crack in every one of its glass panels. There were faded flyers for businesses selling everything from carpets to sex stuck to the wall behind the pay phone.

Jake's call had to be patched through via an operator in Delhi, but after a few rings he heard a familiar voice.

"Hello?"

"Will? Will, is that you?"

"Jake? Where the hell are you guys?"

Will's voice was sleepy, Jake knew he'd woken him. He imagined the moon shining bright over the warm Caribbean seas, casting a soft glow over the plantation house on the island of San Sebastian. Jake suddenly felt a million miles away.

"We're at the train station in Islamabad on our way to Saint

The Tomb of Heaven

Petersburg," Jake told him, pulling harder on the door with the broken hinge so that nobody could overhear his conversation. "We've got the Keys to Rasputin's Riddles and didn't want to risk customs confiscating them at the airport. We figured train was a safer way to go."

"Whoa, whoa, slow down. Let me go wake the Professor."

"No, it's you I want to speak to. You're the history major. Tell me everything you know about Rasputin."

"Rasputin? The crazy, religious nut who fucked the Tsar's wife?"

"That's a good start. Let's go from there."

Will let out a deep breath over the phone. Jake could almost hear the cogs in his clever young brain cranking into gear. "Well, let's see. The guy was like a mystic. A spiritual healer. He was a real charmer in a creepy kinda way. Put it this way, if he was alive today he'd have his own TV network and a heavily-guarded headquarters in L.A."

"I get the picture."

"Of course, there was no TV in Russia in the early 1900s, so what better way to exert your power over the people than to cozy up to the Tsar's wife. Why not, right? After all, Alexandra was beautiful, influential and very, very impressionable. She took Rasputin on as her spiritual adviser... among other things, if you catch my drift. He moved into the palace and quickly began interfering in political affairs. This didn't sit well with Russia's monarchists who were concerned that Rasputin would bring about the end of the Romanov royal family. So they killed him..." Will's tone turned mysterious at that point. "Or at least they tried."

"What do you mean?"

A porter pushing a trolley stacked with battered suitcases slammed into the phone booth and Jake jumped. The porter waved an apology to Jake and moved on.

"Go on," Jake urged Will.

"Rasputin was infamous for dabbling in the occult, the supernatural. He surrounded himself with disciples and held secret gatherings. They built altars, they distorted their faith, they practiced rituals that the aristocracy at the time called 'ungodly'. Rasputin himself was obsessed with immortality. He cooked up potions in an attempt to prolong his own life, and concocted poisons to end the lives of his enemies."

"The potions... did they work?"

"Nobody knows for sure. But assassinating Rasputin was easier said than done. It was winter in Russia, 1914, and colder than hell itself. Those conspiring to assassinate Rasputin devised a plan to lure him to the palace of Prince Felix Yussupov, one of the conspirators, on the pretence of healing Yussupov's wife, Princess Irina. There they served Rasputin pastries and wine laced with potassium cyanide. At first Rasputin refused to eat, but he eventually gave in to the wine and proceeded to get himself drunk. Soon he became ill, frothing at the mouth, but the poison didn't kill. Instead it made him suspicious. Then furious. Prince Yussupov panicked, pulled out a revolver and shot him in the chest at close range. Unfortunately for the prince, the bullet didn't kill Rasputin either. The mad monk flew into a rage, attacked the prince then tried to escape. He staggered outside into the snow where his would-be assassins gave chase. They fired a gun at him again as he fled into the night. One bullet hit Rasputin in the back. Another bullet hit him in the head. Rasputin fell to the ground, but when the conspirators reached him he was still breathing, still glaring at them with a demonic look in his eye. They didn't know what to do, so they threw the monk into a river to finish him off. Rasputin crashed through the ice and vanished into the freezing, black waters."

"Did they ever find the body?"

"Days later a body was found, but some say it belonged to one of Rasputin's disciples who had shot himself on the banks of the river, sacrificing his own life so that people would believe Rasputin was dead... when in fact—"

The Tomb of Heaven

"He's very much still alive," uttered Jake as a terrible, sinking feeling filled his gut.

Jake was about to hang up and hurry back to Shane and Daniel who were still on board the train, but before he did he paused a moment, then asked, "Will, how's Eden doing?"

The question was met with an even longer pause from Will. "He's okay. He's had a fever. He's in and out of consciousness. Dr. Dante is on his way from Rome to examine him. The Professor wanted to call in a doctor from the mainland, but Dante insisted he come."

Fear and concern took over Jake's voice. "Maybe I should come back. I can be on a plane first thing tomorrow—"

"Jake, he's gonna be okay. Eden's not going anywhere. He'll be waiting for you when you get home."

Jake smiled. "Home," he said. "I'm starting to like the ring of that. We'll see you in few days."

With that he hung up the phone and shouldered his way out of the booth and into the cold.

Inside their compartment on board the train, Jake paced up and down the tiny space from the train window to the compartment door while Shane and Daniel sat on the compartment's frayed cloth seats studying the different sized Russian dolls.

Outside on the platform, people milled back and forth, loading and unloading suitcases while plumes of steam billowed from beneath the train's engine, warning passengers that the train would soon be leaving Islamabad and continuing on its journey to Saint Petersburg in Russia.

"You think it was Rasputin's disciples who chased us through the bazaar?" Daniel asked.

"Well it sure as hell wasn't the North Koreans," Jake answered. "I have a feeling we're about to start slipping on a few red herrings if we can't figure out where that tomb is. The question is, where the hell do we begin looking?"

"I think Saint Petersburg is the obvious place," answered Daniel.

"Is it? I mean, we have the keys to unlock the Tomb of Heaven, but we have no idea *where* the Tomb of Heaven is. Just because Rasputin and the Romanov royal family lived in Saint Petersburg, it doesn't mean the tomb is there."

"No, but if there are any clues to lead us to the tomb, isn't that the logical place to look?" Daniel asked.

"Not necessarily," Shane said as a new thought dawned on him. He was staring down at one of the dolls in his hand. It was the largest doll, the one depicting the maiden carrying the lantern. "China," he whispered. "This is China."

"Shane, it's wood," Daniel corrected. "The dolls are made out of wood, not china."

"No, that's not what I mean. It's on the dress."

"What the hell are you talking about?" Jake asked.

Shane looked from the largest doll to the other doll in his hand. He glanced at the three dolls that Daniel held. All five of the dolls were painted differently, each of them unique.

Shane looked excitedly at Daniel, then at Jake, then back to the dolls. "What if the dolls aren't just the keys to the five crypt doors of the tomb? What if they're also the key to finding the tomb itself?"

"I'm still not following," Jake said.

"The dolls are all hand-painted. One with a skull, one with a ball of string and key, one with a hammer and a basket of tools, one with a pair of shoes, one with a lantern."

"Obviously they're the clues to the riddles inside the tomb," Daniel said.

"Yes, yes. But what if whoever painted the dolls didn't just draw clues. What if they drew a map to the tomb as well." He pointed to the doll with the lantern. "Look at the dress."

"What about it?"

"It's a map. The blue, the green, the white, they're not just random colors. They're points on a map. Hell, if I know anything it's how to read a map. Look, this blue patch here, it's the exact shape of the Caspian Sea. These green sections are land, stretching from Eastern Europe to Mongolia."

"What's the white?" Daniel asked.

"Peaks. Mountains. The Himalayas, the Karakorum range. It's the rooftop of the world."

"You're talking about an area that's millions of square miles. How is that going to lead us to the tomb? It's a needle in a haystack."

With a loud *chuff*, a cloud of steam shrouded the platform outside. A whistle blew, long and hard, and with a jolt the train slowly chugged into motion.

Shane dropped the doll and it rolled on the floor.

He scrambled to pick it up and make sure it hadn't broken.

The doll was unmarked.

He glanced to the second largest doll, the one depicting the maiden holding the white skull.

"There's five dolls. What if the map on each doll gets closer and closer to the tomb?" he said.

"Like zooming in on a satellite image?" Daniel asked.

"Exactly."

"I hate to break it to you, but satellites didn't exist in 1914," Jake pointed out.

"They didn't have to. They had explorers... and cartographers... and the stars to guide them," Shane replied. He reached over the Daniel and plucked the glasses off his face. He slid them on crooked, trying to see more details in the painted doll. He noticed fine cracks in the skull.

"Here!" he exclaimed. "This is the line of the Himalayas from the Karakoram mountains in Pakistan... through Nepal... and down to Bhutan."

With another jolt the train began to pick up a little more momentum as the people and signs and signal house on the platform passed them by.

Shane grabbed the third doll, the one portraying the maiden carrying the pair of shoes. For the first time they noticed the shoe's laces looked as though they were blowing in a breeze.

They were, in fact, depicting borders.

"Pakistan, India, China," said Shane. "This is a map to the Kashmir province."

He snatched up the fourth doll depicting a maiden with a basket of tools. "The weave in the basket. It's the Karakorum Mountains. This is the Baltoro Glacier to the northwest, the Nubra River to the south, and right here is K2, the second highest mountain in the world. And if I'm not mistaken..."

He grabbed the fifth and smallest doll. Squinting at the ball of string in the maiden's hand he saw the intricate markings of two mountain peaks with a narrow pass between them.

"*This* is the Karakoram Pass," Shane said, looking quickly at Daniel and Jake. "We don't need to go to Saint Petersburg. We need to get to Kashmir."

Jake looked out the window as the platform slipped from view and the train began to pick up speed. "We're on the wrong train."

Shane seized the backpack and yanked it open.

Daniel threw the Russian dolls into the pack while Jake pulled open the compartment door.

The three barreled down the corridor of the carriage and hauled open the door at the end of the carriage. The sound of the wheels clacking on the tracks filled the carriage.

A ticket collector caught sight of them and blew his whistle.

But Jake, then Daniel, then Shane were already gone, jumping out of the carriage and onto the side of the tracks as the train continued to build momentum, journeying off in the direction of Saint Petersburg.

Helping each other to their feet, Jake, Shane and Daniel looked back at the station behind them.

They all realized at once that the chill in the breeze was nothing compared to the temperatures they were about to experience.

Shane took a deep breath. "I think we're gonna need some warmer clothes."

5

THE KARAKORAM PASS, KASHMIR

THE RAILWAY LINE meandered higher and higher through the mountains while *The Karakoram Express* gained more and more altitude with every *clackety-clack* of its wheels on the tracks.

Outside, the occasional patch of snow on the ground had turned to fields of ice.

White peaks began to multiply in the distance.

Shane and Daniel had both fallen asleep to the gentle rock and sway of the train journey. Shane's head rolled back and forth on Daniel's shoulder, and a string of drool had left a pool of moisture on Daniel's jacket.

Jake didn't have the heart to wake them as he watched the two of them cozy in to one another, their newly bought fleece-lined jackets swishing against each other as Shane's right arm limply tried to wrap itself around Daniel while he slept. He simply let Shane dribble lovingly on Daniel until the train pulled into the deserted station at Karakoram Pass.

"Guys, wake up. This is it," said Jake, as he picked up the backpack and shook them both by the knee.

The extreme cold hit them immediately as the three of them stepped off the train.

The Tomb of Heaven

There was no protection from the wind.

The station was nothing but a concrete platform with a single sign that read *Karakoram Pass* in four different languages.

There was no station house, nobody to greet them.

The platform was completely empty but for them.

Beyond it was a moonscape, a desolate stretch of gray rocks and ice patches.

As the train chugged away into the distance, the sound of its wheels rambling along the tracks grew fainter and fainter, replaced by the howl of the razor-sharp wind that cut through the narrow pass between two mountains a mile or so away.

"The Karakorum Pass," said Shane. "Let's hope I'm not wrong about this."

The men zipped up their jackets, buried their hands deep in their pockets, and began the trek across the barren plain sloping up to the pass.

Halfway there, Shane glanced over at Daniel then pulled him to a halt.

"What is it?" Daniel asked, his breath short and steaming.

"Your nose is bleeding," said Shane, wiping icy trickles of blood from under Daniel's nose. "Don't worry, it's the altitude. We're almost 18,000 feet above sea level. That's why you're so short of breath."

He moved to continue on, but Daniel caught him by the arm.

"Shane, wait."

Shane stopped.

"What do you think we're going to find up there?" Daniel asked, a look of apprehension and fear in his eyes.

Shane shook his head. "I don't know. Just promise me you'll stay close."

The fear seemed to go away, at least for a moment, and Daniel kissed him, their blue lips warming each other momentarily. "I can manage that," he answered.

When they reached the pass itself, they were surprised how

narrow it was. At less than a hundred and fifty feet wide, you could almost throw a football from one side to the other.

The wind was strong, all of its power channeling through the narrow passageway.

Jake had to shout to be heard. "If there's a cave entrance here somewhere, don't you think someone would have stumbled upon it by now."

"The entrance could be as small as a narrow crevasse in the side of the mountain," shouted Shane back. "Rasputin didn't go to all this trouble for someone to stumble upon the tomb. He wanted us to work for it. He wanted us to follow the clues."

At that moment, Daniel called out from a short distance away. "Shane! Jake! Over here."

They hurried over to find Daniel brushing ice from a boulder that stood waist-high. "I think it's a carving," he said, pointing to a crude etching in the rock.

"It's a carving of a maiden. A Russian maiden," said Jake.

Shane quickly looked around. "There'll be five of them. There'll be five of them in a line pointing to the entrance of the tomb."

He saw another boulder a short distance away, slightly bigger than the first, and ran towards it. He scraped away a sheet of ice to reveal a second maiden.

Jake was already up ahead of him, following the line of the first two boulders to find the same carving on an even bigger boulder. "We've got a third maiden," he shouted over the wind.

"And a fourth," shouted Daniel a moment later, wiping the ice from a larger fourth boulder in the line of rocks.

The three of them all looked in the direction of a fifth boulder, this one as tall as a man.

They bolted towards it.

Their hands frantically pushed and rubbed at the rock's ice-sheeted surface to reveal a fifth Russian maiden.

"It's here," panted Shane. "The entrance is here."

The Tomb of Heaven

The three of them looked around and saw nothing but their barren, rocky surroundings.

"Where exactly?" asked Daniel.

Shane shook his head and walked in a circle. "I don't get it. The clues add up. It makes sense. The entrance to the tomb should be right here."

He stamped his foot on the ground as hard as he could.

Suddenly, a few pebbles beneath him rattled and disappeared —

—before a huge fissure opened up in the earth directly below him.

Shane gasped as the ground swallowed him whole.

Rocks and dirt slid after him into the large crack that just opened in the earth.

"Shane!" shouted Daniel and Jake at the same time, both of them diving onto their stomachs at the edge of the crevasse and peering into the darkness below.

Jake rifled through the backpack for one of the eighteen-inch heavy-duty flashlights they'd bought along with their mountaineering jackets.

He shone the beam of light into the pitch black chasm. "Shane! Shane, can you hear me?"

"Yeah," came the spluttering reply from below.

The beam caught Shane as he was picking himself up out of the rubble and dusting himself off. That's when he seemed to catch sight of something else in the dark.

"Say, do you wanna toss one of those flashlights down?"

Jake pulled a second flashlight from the backpack and dropped it into the hole.

Shane caught it, flicked it on and shone the light through the darkness. After a moment, he looked up with a smile on his dusty face.

"You guys might wanna get your asses down here," he said. "We just found ourselves the entrance to the Tomb of Heaven."

Jake and Daniel descended the rock walls leading into the cavern with care, making sure not too slip and fall this close to the end of their quest.

When they were almost at the bottom, Jake thought he heard a distant noise from above—a *thump-thump-thump* that cut through the howling wind above them.

"Did you hear that?" he asked Daniel.

Daniel stopped his climb, listened and shook his head. "Hear what?"

The sound was gone. "Nothing," replied Jake.

At that moment, Daniel's foot slipped. Rocks cascaded as he lost his grip altogether. Desperately he tried to grab onto something to stop his fall, but before he could hit the ground Shane was there to catch him.

As Daniel fell into his arms, Shane asked in a panic, "Are you okay?"

Daniel nodded. "Yeah, I'm fine. Just as clumsy as ever, that's all."

Jake made a final jump from the rock wall and landed beside them while Shane eased Daniel to his feet.

Daniel rubbed his eyes, trying to adjust to the dark.

"Here," Jake said, digging the third flashlight out of the backpack and handing it to Daniel. "You're gonna need this."

"Especially if we're going to open that crypt door," added Shane.

He shone his flashlight ahead of them, and Jake and Daniel did the same.

A short distance away, at the end of the cavern, stood a large stone door. It was as least fifteen feet high and twenty feet wide, intricately carved and wet with icy residue that trickled down the cavern walls.

"Nature didn't put *that* there," said Shane.

Cautiously the three of them stepped towards it, the spotlights of their beams dancing over the carvings that decorated the crypt door. In the center of it was a small square alcove that stood eight inches high. Around that were carvings of suns and moons, peasants and kings, demons and fire. And across the top of the door were four sentences written in Russian.

Jake, Shane and Daniel stopped in front of the door, their three flashlights shining on the words inscribed in stone.

"Can you read it?" Shane asked Daniel.

Daniel nodded. "It's a riddle."

He moved one step closer—

—and as he did, a stone slab beneath his feet sank two inches.

"What just happened?" Daniel asked urgently.

In the same moment, they heard a mechanical click followed by a loud groan coming from the right-hand side of the cavern.

The beams of all three flashlights quickly turned to illuminate a giant sandglass fixed to the wall by a mechanical arm which was now slowly turning.

The sandglass rotated forty-five degrees, ninety degrees, one-eighty degrees.

When it tipped upside-down it stopped, letting the sand inside pour into the lower chamber of glass.

"Oh God, it's a timer," breathed Jake, frantically rummaging through the backpack and pulling out the Russian dolls.

"Timer? Davenport didn't say anything about a timer," Daniel said. "How long do we have?"

Shane quickly sized up the amount of sand in the sandglass and how quickly it was pouring into the lower chamber. "Three minutes, maybe less."

"What happens then?"

"My guess would be the lock to this door closes forever," answered Jake, catching the wooden dolls as they rolled across the cavern floor in his panic to get them out.

Shane grabbed Daniel by the arm and pointed to the inscription above the door. "The riddle, what does it say?"

Daniel quickly gulped back his fear, the beam of his flashlight moving from one word to the next as he translated the inscription—

"I have a tongue but cannot talk. I trek the earth but cannot walk. I have a soul but do not pray. You'll take me to your grave some day."

Jake cradled the five dolls in his arms, glancing quickly from one to the other to the next.

The maiden holding the lantern.

The maiden carrying the shoes.

The maiden holding the basket of tools.

The maiden carrying the ball of string and key.

The maiden holding the skull.

Which doll was the key to the riddle?

Which doll was the *right* doll?

"The skull. It's gotta be the one with the skull," said Jake.

"Why?" asked Shane.

"Death! The riddle mentions going to the grave. It's about death."

Jake grabbed the doll with the skull and moved toward the alcove in the door.

Shane pulled him back. "Jake, we've only get one shot at this. If we get the answer wrong—if we put the wrong key into the lock—the door stays closed forever."

"And if we run out of time, what happens then?" Jake asked, glancing over at the sandglass.

More than half the sand had already emptied into the lower chamber.

Jake moved toward the door again but Shane held him back once more.

"Daniel, read out the riddle again. And hurry."

Daniel took a deep breath and hastily blurted, "I have a tongue but cannot talk—"

"Skulls once had a tongue but can't talk anymore," said Jake.

He moved closer to the door, but the next line stopped him.

The Tomb of Heaven

"I trek the earth but cannot walk," translated Daniel.

Jake hesitated, mere inches from placing the maiden with the skull into the alcove.

Shane glanced at the sandglass. They had a minute, perhaps even less, remaining.

"I have a soul but do not pray," continued Daniel. "You'll take me to your grave some day."

Jake held the doll with the skull over the alcove.

"Wait!" exclaimed Shane. "It's not about death. It's the maiden with the shoes!"

Jake pulled back from the door.

Shane took the doll depicting the maiden carrying the shoes from Jake's arms. "I have a tongue but cannot speak," said Shane. "Shoes have a tongue. They trek the earth but they can't walk unless you're wearing them. They have a sole underneath, but they sure as hell don't pray. And when someone dresses you for your funeral, you'll be wearing them to your grave some day."

Shane grinned, relieved.

Jake wiped the sweat from his brow. "Shit that was close."

They both glanced at the sandglass with seconds to spare before Shane stepped up to the door, his hand shaking as he moved to place the maiden carrying the shoes into the alcove.

"No!" cried Daniel, suddenly leaping at Shane from the side and crash-tackling him to the ground, sending the doll clattering over the cavern floor.

"What the hell are you doing?" Shane gasped in wide-eyed shock.

"It's the cobbler," Daniel uttered. "The maiden carrying the basket of tools. She's a cobbler! The knife, the hammer, the parchment of *leather*! She makes shoes! It's not about the maiden carrying the shoes, it's about the one who *makes* them!"

Shane shone his flashlight at the sandglass to see the last grains of sand trickling through.

Jake emptied his arms of the dolls, all but the one depicting the maiden with the basket of tools.

He lunged for the crypt door.

The last grains of sand poured through the sandglass.

Jake slid the Russian doll into the alcove.

The three of them froze and held their breath.

At first nothing happened.

There was silence but for the *drip-drip-drip* of water running down the cavern walls.

Then—

—with a heart-stopping *SNAP!*—

—the alcove slammed shut, pulverizing the wooden doll inside.

Jake, Shane and Daniel all scrambled several feet back from the door.

"Oh God, I think we broke it," said Daniel.

Then, with a loud rumbling sound, the door began to move.

It opened from the center, the left and right sides of the door sliding apart to reveal a corridor that was perhaps twenty, thirty, forty feet long. The doors were in fact walls, sliding into the sides of the cavern to make a passageway that opened before them.

"Gentlemen, I do believe the first crypt door is now open," said Jake.

Collecting the remaining four dolls in their arms, Jake, Shane and Daniel cautiously made their way along the now wide-open passage.

That's when they all heard a mechanical click and a groan somewhere up ahead.

"Another sand-glass," Jake said. "The second timer's already started."

The three of them broke into a sprint as they bolted along the wide passage and emerged into a second cavernous chamber similar to the first.

The Tomb of Heaven

Sure enough a sandglass on the right side of the cavern had already turned, the sand quickly filling the lower chamber.

"The first door must have activated it," said Jake as his flashlight shone from the sandglass to the inscription above the second crypt door. "No pressure, Daniel, but the sands through the hourglass are like the minutes of our lives right now!"

Daniel pointed the beam of his light on the inscription and read aloud—

"I touch the earth. I touch the sky. But if I touch you, you'll surely die."

Jake, Shane and Daniel all turned to each other.

"What touches the earth and sky?" Shane asked frantically.

"Air," said Jake with a shrug.

"Rain," suggested Daniel.

"Sunlight," offered Shane. He fumbled through the dolls and pulled out the one with the lantern. "Light is everywhere. Sunlight. Moonlight. It touches everything."

He stepped toward the door with the doll, then paused, pondering his answer and how close they came to being wrong the last time.

He turned back to Jake and Daniel, before the three of them glanced over at the sandglass. The top chamber was already half empty, the bottom chamber filling up fast.

Daniel shone his beam on the inscription once more. "I touch the earth. I touch the sky. But if I touch you, you'll surely die." He asked the question, "What touches the sky that can kill you."

In unison, all three men answered, "Lightning!"

The grains continued to slide swiftly through the sandglass.

Jake, Shane and Daniel looked from one doll to the other.

The maiden holding the skull.

The maiden carrying the shoes.

The maiden carrying the ball of string and key.

The maiden holding the lantern.

Which doll was the key to the riddle?

Which doll was the *right* doll?

"The shoes," Daniel said desperately. "It's the maiden with the shoes."

"That's what we thought last time and it was wrong," argued Jake.

"If your shoes have rubber soles the lightning can't kill you," Daniel said, trying to justify his reasoning. "She's taken her shoes off. Surely she'll die."

Jake looked at Daniel, unconvinced, then at the sandglass.

They had thirty seconds of sand left, perhaps less.

"Wait!" said Shane. "It's not just about lightning. It's about being struck by lightning! The ball of string, the key, the ribbons and bows in the maiden's hair. She's about to fly a kite, just like Benjamin Franklin when he discovered electricity! It's the most famous lightning strike in history."

The three of them looked at the timer.

They had perhaps five seconds left—

—four, three, two—

Shane grabbed the doll with the maiden holding the ball of string and key.

He pushed it inside the alcove in the door, just as the last grain of sand sailed into the lower chamber of the sandglass.

Again, everything in the chamber was still and silent.

Then suddenly—

—*SNAP!*

The alcove slammed shut like a deadly mousetrap.

The doll was pulverized.

And slowly, with a loud rumbling sound, the door began to open.

This time it ascended from the floor into the ceiling, slowly rising to reveal the third chamber.

Again the three men heard the mechanical click and grind of another sandglass turning.

The Tomb of Heaven

"This is getting somewhat relentless," Daniel uttered with an exasperated sigh.

Shane grabbed him by the arm. "We've past the point of no return now, babe. No time to dilly-dally!"

As the three started sprinting, Daniel asked with a smirk, "Did you just call me 'babe'?"

After which Jake asked with a smirk, "Did you just say 'dilly-dally'?"

Shane simply rolled his eyes. "Will you two please focus on the problem at hand?"

The three of them skidded up to the door in the third chamber.

The sandglass was already pouring the seconds away.

Daniel shone his flashlight directly at the inscription and read —

"The more of me there is, the less you see. I'll take hold of your heart, if you give me the key."

The three of them looked at the remaining three dolls.

"The maiden with the key is already gone," said Shane.

"You're thinking too literally," Daniel replied. "If something takes hold of your heart, what does it do?"

"It consumes you," Jake answered. "Good, bad, love, hate, jealousy, desire, hope, loss. If it takes hold of your heart, it becomes you."

Shane turned his flashlight to the sandglass. "Guys, thanks for the free psychology session but we're running out of time here."

Daniel looked at the three remaining dolls.

The maiden holding the skull.

The maiden carrying the shoes.

The maiden holding the lantern.

Which doll was the key to the riddle?

Which doll was the *right* doll?

"Jake's right," Daniel announced. "Good, bad, hope, loss... darkness and light." He shone his flashlight at the inscription again. "The more of me there is, the less you see. The answer is darkness. The all-consuming power of darkness. Rasputin worshipped it."

"We'll be worshipping it too—forever—if you don't unlock the door," warned Shane as the last grains of sand trickled through the sandglass. "Now!"

"The only thing that can fight the dark, is the light," said Daniel.

He shoved the maiden carrying the lantern into the alcove as the sand ran out.

SNAP!

The alcove smashed the doll.

This time the crypt door began to rotate, almost like a revolving door in a department store or hotel lobby. The right side of the door moved inward, while the left side rotated outward. It stopped parallel with the walls, forming an opening on both the left and right sides of the door.

The mechanical click and grind of another sandglass turning echoed from deep within the fourth chamber.

Jake, Shane and Daniel bolted for the next crypt door.

The beam of Daniel's flashlight followed the inscription as he translated—

"The more you take of me, the more you leave behind. Forever I am lost to the winds of time."

The three of them looked at the two remaining dolls.

The maiden holding the skull.

The maiden carrying the shoes.

Which doll was the key to the riddle?

Which doll was the *right* doll?

"What do you take, but leave?" asked Shane.

"I know this one," announced Daniel. "You take steps. Footsteps. And leave your footprints behind you. It's the maiden carrying the shoes."

Daniel took the doll depicting the maiden holding the shoes

and moved toward the door.

Suddenly Jake grabbed Daniel by the arm. "Wait a second."

He wasn't looking at Daniel or the door or the sandglass. He was looking down at his—

"Shoes. The butler's shoes," he murmured.

"Jake? What are you talking about?" asked Shane.

Jake looked at him with alarm. "It's a set-up. This whole thing is a set-up."

"What do you mean?"

"Back in New York, the butler at Davenport's apartment. He was wearing scuffed shoes. No butler wears scuffed shoes. That man wasn't a butler."

"No," said a voice from behind them.

Startled, Jake, Shane and Daniel all spun about and shone their torches on Edgar Davenport standing thirty feet behind them in the chamber.

"You're quite right, Mr. Stone. The man you met at the door wasn't Salinger at all. I am."

"Then who's Davenport?"

The man now claiming to be Salinger, the butler, stepped aside and the flashlight beams fell on a frail old man in a wheelchair. He had an oxygen mask over his mouth and nose, and his deep-set eyes blinked at the light, as though the brightness dizzied him. His skin was covered in lesions and from underneath a woolen hat his thin hair protruding in patches.

With a bony, spidery hand he pulled the oxygen mask down around his neck and said in a raspy, labored voice, "I'm Edgar Davenport. Might I suggest you place the key inside the lock, before time runs out and the door is sealed forever?"

Jake snatched the doll from Daniel and said to Davenport, "Might I suggest you explain yourself or I'll break this damn doll into splinters?"

That's when they heard the cocking of pistols.

They shone their flashlights right and left to see that Davenport and Salinger had an entourage—the three hooded men from Karachi were back in the game.

"May I introduce the last of Rasputin's disciples," said Davenport. "They're very keen to meet their master and won't hesitate to shoot anyone who stands in their path, especially now that you've led us all the way here."

Shane glanced at the sand running through the sandglass. "Jake, the door. Before it's too late."

Jake clenched his jaw and reluctantly turned to the door.

He placed the doll inside the alcove just as the last grain of sand slipped through the sandglass.

The *SNAP!* of the lock crushing the doll echoed like a gunshot through the chamber.

Then with a low groaning sound, the entire door began to slide away.

After a few feet, there was a loud *thunk* and the lower section of the door—perhaps ten inches high—came to stop.

The rest of the door continued to move backward.

There was another *thunk* and the next ten-inch section of the door stopped in place.

Then the next section.

And the next.

"Stairs," Daniel realized aloud. "It's forming a staircase that leads up."

"Up to what?" asked Shane.

"The final riddle," answered Davenport as he watched in awe.

When the last section of the door slotted into place, completing the staircase, Salinger said, "Mr. Stone, please carry Mr. Davenport up the stairs. Mr. Houston and Mr. West, if you wouldn't mind carrying the wheelchair and oxygen tanks, I'm sure we'll all reach the final door before the clock runs out."

With guns trained on him, Jake begrudgingly did as he was ordered and scooped Davenport out of the wheelchair. The old man weighed little more than that of a young girl, his fragile body almost like a bag of bones in Jake's strong arms.

Shane took the oxygen tanks from a rack built into the back of the wheelchair and Daniel picked the chair up off the ground.

With a feeble cough, Davenport spoke as the small group ascended the stairs.

"As you've probably already surmised, there are no North Koreans plotting to steal the elixir."

"And the theft of the fake keys from your trust building in New York?" asked Jake.

"Oh that was real. But the thief was me. Stealing the fake keys was simply a decoy to throw everyone off my scent. The fact is, I'm dying. This is my last chance to not only live… but live forever. I've searched for this tomb my entire life, at least until the cancer got the better of me and forced me into seclusion. But there's nothing like a terminal diagnosis to really get one motivated. My original plan was to hire Rasputin's disciples to find the tomb, but they take orders better than they unravel clues. Of course, realizing that Professor Fathom's men were the only ones who might be capable of thwarting my efforts, I tried to have you killed. But Dr. Moreau proved a poor assassin… and paid the price. When you turned up at my penthouse asking questions, I thought to myself, if you can't beat them, employ them. I had the newspaper delivery boy pose as my butler, while Salinger posed as me. After all, meeting a man in my state would have given the game away, don't you agree?"

They reached the top of the staircase and stood before the fifth and final crypt door.

It was taller than any of the other doors, and its carvings more gruesome, depicting beheadings, disembowelments and all manner of violent torture—as though warning anyone who came near that hell itself was just on the other side.

With guns still pointing at them, Daniel set the wheelchair down and Shane replaced the oxygen tanks.

Jake lowered the brittle old man back into his chair. "How did you find us?"

Davenport took a breath from his oxygen mask then spluttered a little with laughter. "When the disciples followed you to Karachi, you assumed they were there to steal the dolls when in fact their mission was to attach a tracking device to your backpack."

He pointed to a small black object, no bigger than a ladybird, pinned to one strap of the pack on Jake's back.

Jake angrily pulled the pack off his shoulders and threw it to the ground.

The old man cackled till he almost couldn't breathe.

Salinger came to his aid, securing the oxygen mask over his mouth and nose. "Enough talk," he told Jake before gesturing to the last sandglass with a nod of his head. "Time's almost up. Open the door."

Daniel shone his flashlight on the inscription above the door and read—

"What the beggar has, and the rich require. What all contented men desire. What misers spend and spendthrifts save. And all men carry to the grave."

Jake took the last doll in his hand and stood before the alcove as the last few seconds of sand spilled through the sandglass. The skull in the maiden's hand seemed to stare back at him.

Davenport pulled the oxygen mask away once more and breathed, "The answer is nothing. Death... is nothing. Eternal life... is everything."

The sand ran out just as Jake sat the final doll in place.

SNAP!

Somewhere behind the door they heard the grinding of stone wheels.

A seal broke at the top of the door, sending small rocks and dirt sliding down the stone surface.

The door was lowering like a drawbridge until, with a solemn *thump*, the top of the enormous door came to rest on the other side of a black chasm.

The men shone their flashlights to the chamber on the opposite side. There was what looked like a stone altar. Beside it, almost exactly the same size, was a stone sarcophagus with no lid.

"Good God, this just gets creepier," uttered Daniel.

"I don't think God has anything to do with this place," said Shane.

Sitting on top of the altar, Davenport noticed a large silver decanter encrusted with jewels. It had a flat, wide base, a handle on one side, and a tall, narrow spout. It looked almost like a Genie's bottle from some Arabian tale, but what it contained was more powerful than any spirit.

Davenport's dying eyes widened with hope. "The elixir of life," he whispered.

Jake shone his beam on the door now spanning the chasm like a drawbridge. He picked up a loose rock from the ground and through it into the abyss beside the bridge. There was no sound of the rock hitting the ground.

Davenport looked at him and grinned. "You first, Mr. Stone. I insist."

The guns pointed at him waved him toward the drawbridge, urging him to do as he was told.

Slowly Jake stepped up to the door.

It stretched twenty feet long from one side of the chasm to the other, and was no more than eight feet wide. It was not an impossible crossing to make, but the stone surface was wet and one slip could send Jake tumbling over the edge.

Cautiously he made his way onto the structure, walking over the carvings of heads skewered on lances and peasants being burned at the stake. The sight of it was sickening, so he looked ahead instead, pointing the beam of his flashlight at the altar and focusing his attention on the glittering silver decanter until soon he made it safely to the other side.

Daniel was next to cross the drawbridge, followed by Shane.

The three disciples made it across next, and last of all, Salinger pushed Davenport in his wheelchair until everyone stood in the last cavernous chamber with the altar and sarcophagus in front of them and the black, bottomless abyss to their backs.

Davenport took one final breath from the oxygen mask, then removed it for the last time.

"This is the moment I've longed for. Immortality. Finally, it's mine." Quivering with anticipation, the frail old man pointed to the decanter. "Salinger, bring me the elixir of life. Bring it to me and I will share it with you, so you can be my loyal and humble servant for all eternity."

Salinger stepped up beside the wheelchair and smiled at the old man. "Sir, I'm honored..." Suddenly the smile fell away from his face. "... but I had other plans."

With that, the butler pulled a pistol from his jacket pocket, placed it against Davenport's temple and promptly blew the old man's brains out.

Everyone jumped as the shot rang out.

Davenport's brittle body jolted then slumped to one side in his chair.

Jake, Shane and Daniel stared in shock as they watched blood, brains and bone fragment ooze from the exit wound in Davenport's skull.

The three disciples took a cautious step back.

"So close, but no cigar," Salinger said before letting out a long sigh. "Oh, what a relief. Now that that's done, it's time to live forever."

Determinedly Salinger stepped up to the altar.

He eyed the bejeweled silver decanter for a moment, then glanced over at the open sarcophagus beside the altar.

Inside it laid none other than Rasputin himself. He was tall

The Tomb of Heaven

and dressed in a frayed old monk's robe. His eyes were closed and his beard had grown all the way down to his knees. His arms were crossed over his beard and chest, and his fingernails were long and curled like a pig's tail.

Without another moment's hesitation Salinger reached for the decanter, then said to the motionless body in the sarcophagus. "This is mine now. I've fucking earned it."

He snatched the decanter off the altar.

"Salinger, wait," called Shane. "You don't know what you're doing."

"On the contrary, Mr. Houston. I know exactly what I'm doing. I'm about to take my place amongst the gods."

With that he raised the spout of the decanter to his lips and poured the elixir of life into his mouth, guzzling greedily until he saw out of the corner of his eye—

—the formidable shape of Rasputin sit suddenly upright in his sarcophagus, his dark eyes filled with rage and his rotted teeth clenched in fury.

With a sweep of his long, powerful arm Rasputin knocked the decanter out of Salinger's hands then sent the butler flying through the air.

With a grunt Salinger slammed into a wall of the chamber and collapsed to the ground.

Rasputin let out a roar, and with a leap that almost seemed impossible he launched himself out of the sarcophagus and landed with an almighty thud on the cavern floor.

Everyone instantly backed up, all except one of the disciplines who fell to his knees before his master.

The towering form of Rasputin locked eyes on the hooded man and lunged at him, seizing disciple's head in the large, claw-like hands.

The disciple screamed and dropped his gun.

The weapon rattled across the floor toward Jake.

Rasputin lifted the disciple off his feet then buried his face inside the man's hood.

The disciple's body began to convulse, and a moment later Rasputin pulled his head out of the hood. He was covered in blood, with half of the disciple's face dangling from his mouth as he chewed and chomped on the human flesh.

"Oh fuck," uttered Shane. "Time to go!"

Rasputin hurled the disciple over the edge of the abyss, then turned his attention to Jake.

Jake looked from the gun near his feet to the body of Davenport slumped in the wheelchair.

In one swift move he seized the wheelchair and pushed it as hard as he could in Rasputin's direction.

The chair rattled across the rocky floor of the cavern while Rasputin laughed at the feeble attempt to stop him.

He seized the chair as it ran into his shins, lifting it off the ground—Davenport and all—to throw at Jake.

The mad monk held it high over his head and gave another guttural roar.

That's when Jake dived to the ground, snatched up the gun, and took one clear shot at the oxygen tanks strapped to the back of the chair.

The bullet punctured one of the tanks—

—and an almighty explosion ripped through the chamber, sending a tremor through the earth as Rasputin, Davenport and the chair erupted in a ball of fire.

The blast knocked everyone to the ground.

It also triggered the mechanics inside the five crypt doors, all of each began to close.

Slowly the drawbridge door began to lift off the ground.

Salinger saw it first, quickly shaking himself to his senses and bolting for the ascending bridge.

He had drunk the elixir.

He knew if he didn't escape the tomb, he'd be trapped inside for all eternity.

The Tomb of Heaven

The door lifted a foot off the ground and Salinger jumped onto it.

One of the remaining disciples leapt onto the door at the same time, almost knocking Salinger over.

"Get out of my way!" Salinger snapped, before shoving the disciple over the edge of the drawbridge—

—and into the bottomless abyss.

The man's horrified scream echoed through the chamber as he sailed into the darkness, vanishing forever.

The third disciple hurriedly leapt onto the door, following swiftly behind Salinger but cautious not to get in the man's way as they made their escape from the chamber.

Hurriedly, Shane pulled himself to his feet and grabbed Daniel by the arm. "Come on!"

Daniel shoved his flashlight into his belt and jumped onto the rising door, but as Shane glanced back at the fire still burning from the blast, he saw Jake—who was closest to the explosion—had been knocked unconscious by the eruption.

Shane slid to the ground beside Jake.

He sat him up and slapped his cheeks to try and wake him.

"Jake, wake up. We gotta go!"

Jake groggily opened his eyes, but as soon as he saw his surroundings he snapped into action, trying to pull himself to his feet.

Shane helped him up and assisted him to the edge of the abyss.

The drawbridge was now five feet off the ground and moving farther away by the second.

"Can you jump?" Shane asked Jake.

Jake nodded, took an unsteady step backward, then leapt for the drawbridge.

He managed to grab the edge of the drawbridge with his hands and get his elbows up over the edge before Daniel grabbed him and hauled him up.

"Jump, Shane! Jump now!"

As the drawbridge inched higher, Shane took a running jump.

His fingers hooked the edge of the rising door—just.

Both Daniel and Jake reached down and grabbed an arm each, but as they did so, a howl of pain and anger filled the chamber.

Shane turned his head to see the fiery figure of Rasputin charge from the blaze and leap for the drawbridge.

But the burning monk did not grab hold of the bridge.

He grabbed hold of the dangling frame of Shane.

With the sudden weight pulling him down, Shane lost his grip, his fingers slipping off the edge.

Daniel and Jake tightened their hold on Shane's forearms, catching him before he plunged into the abyss.

Burning and smoldering—his long beard ablaze and his robe turning to cinders—Rasputin cackled and tried to claw his way up Shane's body.

The heat from the fire scorched Shane's clothes as he tried to kick the mad monk off him.

The drawbridge rose higher and higher, ascending to a forty-five degree angle, then fifty, then sixty.

Daniel and Jake tried their hardest to pull Shane up and over the edge, but the weight of Rasputin—struggling and scratching and snaking his way up Shane's frame—made it almost impossible.

"Shane, you have to climb! You have to pull yourself up!" shouted Daniel.

The door was mere seconds from closing shut.

Daniel and Jake were now holding on so as not to slide down the other side.

"I can't... reach..." panted Shane.

Shane slipped another inch away from the edge.

His fingers were now clutching Daniel's fingers in one hand and Jake's in the other, but they were losing their grip.

Daniel peered over the edge at Shane.

The Tomb of Heaven

Suddenly the large clawed hand of Rasputin grabbed the top of Shane's skull and the monk's grinning face appeared above Shane's head, leering at Daniel.

Shane could smell the hot, stinking breath of the mad monk.

He felt the burning beard scorch the back of his neck.

That's when Shane let out a cry of pain, barely able to hold on any longer.

At that moment, Daniel had had enough.

He bunched up his fist.

He pulled his arm back.

And throwing one punch after another after another straight into the hooked nose of Rasputin, he demanded, "Get your evil... filthy... Russian... hands... off... my... boyfriend!"

Daniel delivered the last punch as hard as he could.

For a moment, Rasputin held on.

But as his eyes rolled back into his head, his claws slipped off Shane, and with that Rasputin let go and fell into the abyss.

The mad monk's smoldering robe flapped in the air as Rasputin plummeted into the darkness—

—never to be seen again.

A second later, Daniel and Jake grabbed a firm hold of Shane and with all their might they yanked him up and over the edge, seconds before the drawbridge sealed shut forever.

The three of them fell from the top of the door all the way to the ground, landing with a grunt and rolling across the floor of the next cavern.

But their escape wasn't over yet.

"The staircase," said Jake, looking ahead to see the stairs transforming back into a door.

Jake, Shane and Daniel bolted for the quickly closing gap, the stairs now steep and only inches apart.

They threw themselves down the stairs, tumbling and toppling and crashing down the almost vertical steps just as the gap at the top sealed completely.

Up ahead they saw Salinger making his way toward the slowly closing rotating crypt door.

Following right behind him was the last disciple—

—until a rumble like a freight train shook the entire tomb, an aftershock from the explosion.

Rocks and rubble rained from the ceiling of the cavern, then a huge boulder dislodged itself and fell directly on top of the last disciple, crushing him before he could even scream.

As the ripple of the tremor continued to shake the cavern, Jake, Shane and Daniel leapt to their feet and sprinted for the rotating door, racing around the fallen boulder with the splattered disciple underneath it.

Jake bolted through the right side of the rotating door.

Shane and Daniel squeezed through the left side.

With a heavy thud the door sealed shut behind them.

Ahead they saw the second last door descending from the ceiling.

Salinger ducked his head slightly as he ran beneath the closing door, making an easy escape. He looked back and laughed, then disappeared into the final chamber.

Jake, Shane and Daniel poured on the speed, running as fast as they could for the descending door.

Another rumble rocked the cavern.

Jake threw himself at the ground and rolled under the door with only a few feet to spare.

Shane dived onto his stomach and scrambled through in a commando crawl.

He turned back as Daniel hurled himself onto the ground.

Shane grabbed the reporter's jacket and yanked him through just as the door clipped Daniel's heel and slammed shut.

There was one more door to get through, the slowly closing corridor.

It was a door that Salinger would never pass through, for only a few feet short of the closing corridor walls, Salinger was now

The Tomb of Heaven

pinned against the cavern wall by a boulder that had come loose from the ceiling and rolled across the chamber.

He was still very much alive, but his entire left side was caught between the rock and the cavern wall.

Jake, Shane and Daniel hurried toward him.

"Help me," Salinger begged. "Get me out of here."

For a desperate moment, Jake, Shane and Daniel tried to move the boulder, pushing with all their might. But no matter how hard they tried, they couldn't budge the giant rock.

Shane glanced at the closing corridor and said, "Jake, we have to go now. Or none of us are getting out of here."

Shane grabbed Daniel and together they raced for the closing walls.

Jake lingered a moment longer. Perhaps a moment too long. "For all it's worth," he said to Salinger, "I hope you enjoy eternity. So close, but no cigar."

With that he sprinted for the corridor.

Salinger screamed after them. "No!!! Don't you dare leave me!!"

Daniel and Shane dashed along the corridor as it grew narrower and narrower, threatening to crush them if they didn't make it out in time.

Daniel raced from the closing gap and out to safety first.

Shane's shoulders brushed the closing walls as he too leapt out of the corridor.

But when they looked back, they saw Jake had no hope of making it out alive.

He raced into the corridor but still had thirty feet to go before he had to turn on his side to squeeze though.

"Faster, Jake! Faster!" shouted Shane.

Jake tried to move as fast as he could, closing the distance to his escape. But the gap between the walls was down to inches now.

"He's not gonna make it," Daniel breathed in a panic. "We

need to jam it with something." He desperately looked around for something to stop the walls from closing.

Jake had twenty feet to go.

Fifteen feet.

Daniel suddenly remembered the eighteen-inch flashlight tucked in his belt.

He pulled it out, and just as the walls moved to within eighteen inches of one another, Daniel slid the flashlight between them.

There was a loud groan from within the walls as the doors stopped momentarily and the mechanics strained.

Almost immediately the heavy-duty flashlight began to buckle.

"Hurry, Jake! Hurry!"

Jake was struggling along as quickly as he could, his broad shoulders and large chest scraping the stone walls as he squeezed through.

The shaft of the flashlight cracked in several places and the walls crunched it down by an inch or two.

Jake was almost through.

Shane and Daniel both reached in and grabbed his forearms.

The mechanics whirred and growled.

The flashlight snapped.

At the last second, Shane and Daniel yanked Jake out of the corridor of death just as the two walls slammed together, destroying the flashlight—

—and sealing Salinger inside the tomb for all time.

6

THE ISLAND OF SAN SEBASTIAN, THE CARIBBEAN SEA

THE SUN DANCED on the crystal waters of the Caribbean as the Jake, Shane and Daniel stepped out of a water taxi and onto the island jetty to be greeted by a round of hugs.

Elsa was first to throw her arms around the boys. *"Mein Gott!* You boys must be starving!"

"Actually, we ate on the plane," said Shane.

"Don't be ridiculous. Airplane food is *not* real food. I have a *schupfnudel* cooking as we speak, although I had better go rescue it before Big Zettie ruins my masterpiece. That woman will be the death of me!"

As Elsa scurried away, Luca, Will and Sam each embraced their friends before Professor Fathom stepped up to them.

"It's good to have you home safe," he said, squeezing Jake and Shane by the forearm. "And Daniel, thank you for your help… and welcome to San Sebastian. Will you be staying long?"

Daniel glanced at Shane. "Hopefully."

"I'm afraid we've run out of spare rooms, but I'm sure you and Shane can make some arrangements." Despite his blindness, the Professor turned to give Shane a wink. "In the meantime, you're just in time for morning tea. We're serving Earl Grey."

"My favorite," said Daniel.

"I know," smiled the Professor.

"He knows everything," whispered Shane into Daniel's ear.

"I heard that. Now hurry along all of you. There are no excuses for being late for tea."

Everyone except Jake and the Professor made their way along the jetty.

Jake could no longer hide his anxiety. "How's Eden doing?"

The Professor could no longer hide his concern. "I must be honest with you. He doesn't quite seem… himself. You should go to him."

Jake didn't waste a single moment.

He found Eden asleep in his downstairs room in the east wing of the plantation house. Gently he sat beside Eden on the bed. He didn't intend to wake him, but in a way he was glad he did.

To see Eden open his eyes—to see him recognize Jake's face and give a smile, no matter how faint—made Jake's heart swell with hope.

"Hey, sleepy head. How you doin'?"

"I'm okay," Eden sighed. "How are you?"

"Glad to be home. I hear the doctor's coming to see you."

"All the way from Rome. I guess something must be up."

"Nothing's up. Everyone just wants you to make a full recovery as fast as possible, that's all. We want nothing but the best doctors in the world for you."

Eden's smile broadened, and Jake rubbed Eden's forearm affectionately.

As soon as he did, Eden winced in agony and sat bolt upright in bed, biting back a scream of pain.

Jake let go of his arm and took Eden firmly by the shoulders in case he was about to have a seizure. "Eden, what is it? Is it your arm? Where's the pain?"

Eden clamped his jaws shut and spat, "It's… everywhere. It's… inside me!"

The Tomb of Heaven

At that moment, Elsa and Big Zettie came rushing into the room. Big Zettie was already filling a syringe with clear liquid from a bottle. Elsa ushered Jake back and Big Zettie administered the injection.

"The doctor sent us morphine to keep him comfortable... until we know more about what's going on."

She slid the needle from his arm and almost immediately a wave of calm came over Eden's face. A moment later he was once again unconscious.

Elsa fanned herself with her apron, as if trying to shoo her worries away. "Until Dr. Dante arrives, all we can do is ease his pain. Come, let him rest now."

The women led a concerned Jake from the room.

He excused himself from morning tea.

He took a shower, but the fears he held for Eden did not wash away.

All he could hear in his head was that scream of pain trying to escape Eden's gritted teeth.

All he could hear was the hammering of his own fearful heart.

All he could hear were the words—

—*It's inside me.*

THE ADVENTURE CONTINUES...

There is a lost temple that can change time as we know it, and there is one man who will destroy everything and anyone to know the truth—his name is Caro Sholtez. In his possession are the four pieces of the most powerful mythical clock in the world, and the only person who can stop him from finding the Temple that can unlock Time itself is Professor Fathom.

READ ON FOR A SNEAK PEEK OF

THE TEMPLE OF TIME:
FATHOM'S FIVE BOOK FIVE

OXFORD UNIVERSITY, ENGLAND, 1972

Max.

That was the name on the envelope, written in ink so fresh it was still glistening. Zhang Sen held it tightly in his fist, careful not to let the wind catch it, but also careful not to let his grip crush it.

On the night of his death over forty years from now, Sen would set the envelope alight aboard the Zhang Diamond Express as the train wound its way up into the mountains of Shandong one last time.

This is what the letter inside said—never opened, never read:

My Dearest Max,

I keep laying my palms flat on the desk to stop them from trembling. It doesn't seem to work. But at least now, if you can't read this letter because of my quivering writing, you'll know why. Or at least you have an excuse to pretend you never read it at all.

The truth is I have something I need to tell you. My head and my damn trembling hands think it is a mistake to do so, and if it is, so be it. But another day and my heart will turn to stone if I don't say something, even if it is only on paper. Even if it is illegible. Even if it comes at a price. And here it is—

You stumble across the quadrangle and I smile as you juggle your books and pat your pockets, wondering what you've forgotten in your rush to get to class.

You blink and blame your spectacles when you've had one too many pints at the pub, and I grin and watch you wipe your lenses with the end of your necktie till you think you're sober again.

You fall asleep on the pages of an open book in the library opposite me, and I want to touch my fingers to your temple and feel its pulse. I imagine that's the calmest it ever gets. When you sleep.

And I wonder what you dream of.

Do you dream of me?

As for my own dreams…

Did you know the miners have been on strike for eight weeks now? Prime Minister Teddy's pretending to remain fierce on the matter, yet back home my father doesn't understand the militant sway of the unions. He fears he may have sent me to the wrong country for my education. He fears I may return to China and tip the balance of power with stupid ideas of freedom and workers' rights. In his last letter he asked if I had the dreams of a rebel.

I answered no.

Yet my heart sighed—yes.

Yes, I want to tip the scales.

Yes, I want to shout from the rooftop of Radcliffe stupid ideas of freedom.

And yes, I want to tell you, Max—I love you.

How brave do I have to be to do that? How stupid and arrogant and sure of myself do I have to be to tip that scale? How certain must I be to change everyone else's expectations of me?

To rewrite their perception of me as a child.

To alter their own memories.

To re-draw their wills.

How reckless do I need to be?

How selfish?
Will I lose everything but you?
Will I lose you too?
My head says yes.
My damn trembling hands say yes.
But my heart—it simply doesn't know. It never will, until my shaking hands put this letter in yours. Will you tremble too? Will I be...
Yours forever,
Sen

Anxiously he glanced up at the clock tower overlooking the university quadrangle. The ornate long hand shifted with a heavy mechanical lurch and another minute disappeared. It was already twelve past nine. Max was late, as usual, for Professor Novak's Mesoamerican Studies lecture. Any minute now the young student would come sprinting across the quadrangle, tucking in his shirt and dropping books in his haste to reach the lecture hall at the opposite end of the quadrangle's trimmed green lawn, completely unaware of how perfect he was.

The mere thought of him made Sen sweat on this cold day.

His hands were sticky and he knew he was leaving fingerprint marks on the envelope. He imagined Max discovering these in years to come, after keeping the letter safe in a box of cherished memories and smiling to himself. Would they be together then? How wonderful their lives might be. How filled they were with the promise of love.

Sen smiled to himself.

Suddenly, like a dart flying through the air at every students' favorite pub *The Nag's Head*, 22-year-old Maximilian Fathom came shooting through an archway, his feet bumbling, his arms juggling falling books as he bolted as fast as he could for the closed door to the lecture hall across the quadrangle.

Sen saw him. His heart leapt.

The Tomb of Heaven

His voice called, loud and determined, knowing this was his chance. "Max!"

Halfway across the lawn Max skidded to a halt and turned. "Sen? Please, not now. I'm running late."

Sen hurried to meet him in the middle of the lawn. "I know, I'm sorry, I just had to—"

"I'm not joking, Sen," muttered Max, impatiently looking at his watch then at the clock tower to double check. "Professor Novak is going to crucify me in front of the whole class."

"I'm sorry. I just wanted to give you this."

Sen held the envelope out to Max, his hand shaking just as he knew it would.

Max snatched the envelope without even looking at his name so carefully scribed on it. Without the slightest quiver of his hand.

Instead he shoved it under his arm and blurted breathlessly, "Thanks, I'll look at it later. I have to go." And with that Max continued sprinting across the lawn.

As Sen stood there, frozen, not knowing what to do or say or think, Max turned around and called, "Maybe I'll catch you at the pub later this afternoon?" He didn't wait for an answer before continuing on.

Sen watched him go. Then caught his chilled breath as the envelope slipped from under Max's arm. It twirled through the brisk wind and fell to the ground. Max didn't even know he'd let it slip. He didn't look back. To Sen, he didn't even care. As Max slipped through the doors into the entry of the lecture hall, Sen walked slowly up to the envelope on the ground and picked it up.

In that moment, Sen's heart didn't simply break. It froze.

Standing there with the envelope in his hand, he decided to keep the letter for himself and place it in his own box of memories. But not ones to be cherished. From that moment on, he would find colder treasures to cherish— and darker dreams to hatch.

Max let the door behind him ease shut so as not to make a sound. He was in the entrance to the lecture hall. From here he could hear Professor Novak's thick Czech accent filtering through the second doorway that led directly into the hall, but here in the short corridor between doors, nobody knew Max was late. Nobody needed to know.

If he turned right and headed up the stairs, he could sneak into the back of the lecture hall just as he had done so many times before. If he was lucky the lights might have been dimmed for one of Professor Novak's less than thrilling slideshows. If he was even luckier he might find a spare seat up near the back of the hall and slip into it undetected. And if he were luckier still, the person next to that empty seat would be Caro Sholtez—handsome, ambitious and clever beyond measure. Without a second's hesitation Max quickly and quietly made his way up the stairs. He reached the back entrance to the lecture theater and inched the door open.

He peered into darkness and sighed with relief. Professor Novak was in the middle of a slideshow. He was a tall man in his early fifties wearing a vest and bowtie. He had strong features, classically Eastern European, with a firm jawline and a noble nose. Back in his day there was no doubting how handsome he would have been. Even now he still received the occasional apple left on his desk by a student admirer. Max was not one of them. His eyes were always focused on someone else he admired... a little too much.

At the back of the auditorium, Max pushed the door open a little wider now, his young slender frame slipping inside the hall unnoticed. Down the many tiers of stairs and seats, Professor Novak stood beside a slide projector. On the screen in front of the projector was a photograph of a large stone-carved head. In his Czech accent, the Professor addressed his students.

"Some would argue that the Olmecs' greatest claim to fame was the collection of giant head carvings they left behind. Ladies and gentlemen, the sculptures you see in these slides measure up to twelve feet tall, weigh up to fifty tons each, and were discovered in the jungle all the way from San Lorenzo to Tres Zapotes. All were carved from single blocks of volcanic basalt from the Tuxtlas Mountains, and no two heads are the same. No other Mesoamerican civilization—either before the Olmecs, or after them—created monuments such as these. They're magnificent. Astonishing. Timeless. But if a single one of you so much as dares mention this as the Olmecs' legacy to mankind in your final semester exams, your mark won't just be a fail, it'll be zero, so that you never forget that the Olmecs' true accomplishment—the one thing that makes them unique above all other ancient societies—was the creation of the concept of zero. The Long Count Calendar that everyone attributes to the Maya may well be an invention of the Olmecs. This is a civilization that pre-dates the Mayan world, as well as pre-dates Mayan technology."

As Novak spoke, Max stepped cautiously through the darkness of the theater to the top step.

"Here we have a people who identified the importance of zero. Who realized that the concept of nothingness had infinite meaning and impact."

Max's eyes adjusted to the dark as he spied Caro sitting in a chair by the isle, listening intently. For a second Max thought Caro glanced back at him, smiled at him. But Max couldn't be sure. He saw an empty seat beside Caro and made his way toward it.

From beside the slide projector, Novak switched slides from the stone Olmec Heads to the carvings of the Mayan Calendar. "The question is, if the Olmecs were capable of realizing that zero, the concept of absolute nothingness, had infinite meaning and purpose and impact... what else were they capable of realizing?"

Max stepped toward Caro. He moved as confidently and as quietly as he could to take the seat beside him. That's when Caro's foot nudged out through the dark— straight in front of Max's feet.

Max tripped on Caro's protruding foot on the stair. The books in Max's arm fell and avalanched down the steps of the theater. Max himself teetered, trying to hold his balance before giving in to momentum and gravity—and Caro's warped sense of humor.

He fell forward, hit his chin, toppled sideways, flipped like a pancake, then hit his chin again. *Bang-grunt-bang!* All he could hear in front of him was Professor Novak shouting from the front of the lecture hall, "What's going on! Lights! Lights!" while several stairs behind him, all Max could hear was Caro laughing.

The lights in the hall flicked on like a blast of sunlight. Professor Novak glared up into the auditorium, plucking the spectacles off his face in outrage. Max's chin skidded to a halt several steps down from where Caro had tripped him. His arms and legs were splayed. Several of his books had almost bounced their way all the way down to the auditorium stage.

"Mr. Fathom! Is this how you make an entrance? If you're going to be late, be discreet, for God's sake!"

Max was already trying to pick himself and his pride up off the steps. "Sir, I'm sorry, I—"

"Don't give me excuses or apologies! Just take a seat... now."

"Sir, yes sir, I'm sorry I didn't mean to—"

"I said shut up and sit!"

"Yes sir!" Max scooped up his books as fast as he could, balancing the precarious stack in his arms as he scampered back up the steps and sank into the seat next to the handsome, smirking Caro.

"Best watch where you're going next time, old chap," Caro chuckled quietly.

Red-faced, Max said nothing. He flipped open his notebook and tried his best to avoid the cold glare of Novak.

"Right then," said the Professor turning back to his slides. "As I was saying…"

※

At the end of lecture, the hall filled with the ruckus of books slamming shut and footsteps thundering to the next class. Max turned to Caro. "I best go apologize, don't you think?"

Caro laughed. "Are you joking? You've already made a total arse of yourself, no need for seconds. I'd stay well clear if I were —"

But Max had already packed his things and was scurrying down the steps toward the lectern. He almost tripped over himself again as he brushed past Hester Primrose.

"Hands off, pervert!"

He almost knocked Penelope Brewster's books out of her arms.

"Do you mind!"

He stumbled into those four notorious nerds Ignatius Swinborne, Nicholas Ayres, Reynold Rafferty and the strange young Norwegian, Lars Valhalla, only to receive an impatient shoulder shove back from Ignatius—

"Watch it, Fathom!"

—before almost crashing straight into Professor Novak's lectern.

"Sir, I'm—"

"If you try to apologize one more time, Mr. Fathom, I'll fail you right now on the spot."

Max lowered his head like a scolded pup and began to retreat, leaving the Professor to pack his old leather briefcase with books and notes.

"Listen, Fathom," said Novak as he clipped his briefcase shut. "You're a bright boy. But unless you open your eyes to the world —to your talent—then you'll be falling down steps all your life.

You could do great things with yourself, Max. Why are you wasting precious time?"

"But sir, I study as hard as I can, I swear it."

Professor Novak looked from Max up the steps of the lecture hall. "That's not what I'm talking about."

Max glanced over his shoulder, following the Professor's gaze. He saw Caro standing at the top of the stairs, waiting for him. He turned back to find the Professor had already turned away from the lectern and was leaving the lecture hall.

"Sir, I *will* do great things. I know I will. You'll see."

"Time will tell, Mr. Fathom," said Professor Novak. "Time will tell."

A hand slapped Max on the shoulder. He spun about, startled, to find that Caro was no longer at the top of the stairs but standing right behind him. "I told you not to bother. Come on, let's ditch anthropology today. I know something that'll make you feel better."

"What's that?"

Caro's eyes shone with mischief. "Me."

Max's heart hammered on the inside of his chest as Caro unfastened the buttons on Max's shirt... one at a time. They had returned to Max's room at the dormitory. Max's roommate had left for a three-week trip to Italy the day before, and the pair knew they were guaranteed some privacy. As the buttons came undone one by one, Caro's fingers brushed lightly against the skin of Max's chest and stomach as the shirt slowly opened.

"You're trembling."

"I'm... I..." Max couldn't put his words together.

Caro simply smiled and reached for Max's belt. He untucked the bottom of the shirt from Max's trousers and lifted the shirt off Max's shoulders. Max's torso was trim and pale, his nipples hard and his breath unsteady.

"Relax," Caro said with a self-assurance that made Max even more nervous.

Max nodded his head, although it came across as more of a shudder.

Caro found it amusing. "You've never done this before, have you." It was an observation, not a question.

Max responded anyway, this time with a quick shake of his head.

"Don't worry, I'll be gentle," Caro promised.

He unbuttoned his own shirt. He unbuckled both their belts and unzipped their trousers. He squeezed Max's aching dick inside his briefs and ushered a gentle, adoring moan out of the young man. The grin had not left Caro's face the entire time, it simply spread wider with varying degrees of confidence and control.

As Caro slid Max's briefs down his legs, he knelt into the position Max prayed he would. Max took a deep, quavering breath as Caro wrapped his lips around the head of Max's yearning, erect cock. He was terrified that his nervous, tremulous body might turn Caro away. But Caro's intentions were made more than clear as he took Max's entire dick into his mouth and began sucking, softly at first, but building with intensity with every bob and thrust of his head.

It didn't take long before Max groaned and announced mere seconds before it happened, "I'm coming! I'm—"

As ripples of pleasure and fear and relief sent shivers through his body, Max released a flood of cum into Caro's mouth, groaning loudly as he did so. Caro drank down every last drop that shot from Max's cock. Max thought his legs would buckle as Caro released his cock and licked the stray beads of cum from his lips. But before Max's legs grew too weak, Caro wrapped his arms around him and guided him to the bed.

"Now it's my turn," he said, laying on his back on the bed and easing Max over him so that Max's legs straddled Caro's body.

Caro's cock was large and hard and pointed up toward Max's untouched ass.

"This may hurt. But anything worth experiencing always does."

Max did hurt. The pain seemed to shoot through his entire body, but soon it was followed by a flood of sheer ecstasy, a joy that took hold of each and every nerve and muscle. When the heat of Caro's seed spilled inside him, sending searing volts of energy and a swirl of rapture through him, Max knew that he and Caro would be in each other's worlds for as long as time would permit.

The two young men heaved with pleasure before Max laid beside Caro on his bed, laying his head on his chest with a blissful smile on his face. Max closed his eyes, his body spent.

As he began to drift off to sleep he whispered, "I think I love you, Caro."

Caro waited until Max began to snore softly, then in a barely audible voice replied, "Don't be silly. We're both far too young for that nonsense."

It was dark outside when Max awoke. Something had woken him. He looked around the room. There was no sign of Caro, but the scarf hanging over the door handle was swinging to and fro, indicating that the door had just closed.

Caro had only just left.

Max felt an ache in his chest. It was a physical pain, although he knew nothing was wrong... apart from the fact his hopes had just been crushed. Hopes that after their first time together, he would wake up in Caro's arms; hopes that this was more than just a casual fling; hopes that he wouldn't open his eyes to find

The Tomb of Heaven

himself all alone as he had every day of his life.

Max lay there for a moment, one hand over his heart as though trying to warm it, protect it. But he didn't lay there long. For as much as his heart hurt, it also wanted to know a reason— Why did Caro leave him? Why couldn't he hold him till morning, or at least wake him before he left? Was it shame? Was it someone else? Was it perhaps the fact that Caro didn't really care at all? Or was it something else entirely?

Max jumped out of bed and stepped over to the window. He saw Caro hurrying across the courtyard, his coat buttoned, his collar turned up to keep out the wind. He walked with determination and a clear direction. He checked his watch and quickened his step.

Max dressed as fast as he could, snatching the scarf off the back of the door as he pulled it shut behind him.

His breath puffed in plumes of steam as he sprinted in the direction that Caro had gone. He weaved his way in and out of familiar corners of the university grounds until he caught sight of Caro leaving the campus and heading for the center of town. Max followed, keeping a safe distance and ducking into the shadows or behind trees every time Caro turned around, as though he was checking to make sure nobody was trailing him.

Caro arrived at Oxford train station just as a train was pulling in. Max managed to jump from the platform onto the steps of the last carriage just as the train was pulling out.

He made his way through the train with his head down, scanning the passengers until he spotted the back of Caro's head at the front of one of the carriages. He bought a ticket from the passing conductor and took a seat to watch Caro, making sure he didn't leave his seat until the train's final destination— London.

By the time the train pulled into Paddington station it was well after ten o'clock at night. Caro caught a red double-decker bus to Westminster and sat upstairs. Max caught the same bus and sat downstairs, out of Caro's sight but able to watch for his departure.

At Westminster, Caro briskly descended the spiral stairs that led from the upper level and stepped off the rear exit of the bus. Max jumped off at the last minute, just as the bus was pulling away from the curb. He thought Caro might have heard his shoes hit the pavement. For a second Caro stopped and turned around. Max melted into the shadows of a doorway. Caro saw nothing unusual and kept moving.

Max followed at a more discreet distance. He watched as Caro turned right under the towering gaze of Big Ben. He trailed him as he turned left down a cobblestone alley. He hurried from one darkened doorway to another as Caro finally reached a pub called *The Twelfth Hour* with a depiction of Big Ben on the sign above the door, swinging gently in the cold night wind.

Caro looked behind him one last time.

Max pressed himself into the shadows of a closed tailor shop's doorway.

Caro vanished inside the pub. Max hurried toward *The Twelfth Hour* and pulled open the door. A wave of rowdy laughter, cigarette smoke and jukebox music hit him immediately. As soon as Max stepped into the pub, he spotted a hat and coat stand. He plucked a stranger's hat off the stand, a black trilby that he put on his head, pulling the brim down over his eyes as low as it would go. It was the best disguise he could manage, hoping the fog of smoke would help veil him.

He walked through the noisy crowd as inconspicuously as possible until he saw Caro seated in a booth against a far wall by himself. For a moment Max was tempted to seize his opportunity, to slide into the seat opposite Caro in that booth and ask him why he had left, what was he feeling, was there any hope at all for the two of them. But then he saw Caro tilt his head back, obviously eavesdropping on the conversation in the booth behind him. Max looked at the booth behind Caro and to his surprise

The Tomb of Heaven

saw the faces of five people he knew: Professor Novak and the four notorious nerds, Ignatius Swinborne, Nicholas Ayres, Reynold Rafferty and Lars Valhalla. They were huddled over the table in the middle of the booth. On it were five pints of ale, as well as four other items, each wrapped in frayed cloth. There was also a tattered, leather-bound book on the table with a thick elastic band around it, as though it were so old it needed to be held together. Professor Novak pulled the elastic band off the book, carefully opened the cover and delicately turned several pages.

Max saw a flirting couple leave the booth on the other side of Professor Novak and the four nerds. He skirted the outer edges of the room, hiding behind the other patrons and keeping the hat low, concealing his eyes. He slid into the booth, his back to the others, just as Caro had done in the booth on the other side of Professor Novak's. Max tilted his head back to listen as best he could. He strained to hear Professor Novak's low, whispering voice over the raucous sounds of the pub crowd. The Professor's thick Czech accent was hard to follow at the best of times. In this place, Max could only pick up the occasional phrase here and there, snippets of a conversation that sounded more serious than anything the professor had taught in class.

"From the maps I've been able to... somewhere within the Tuxtla Mountains... must not be... only hope of keeping the world safe... hiding the four pieces of the—"

Suddenly Professor Novak stopped whispering and uttered aloud, "Caro? What are you doing here?"

Max shot a glance over his shoulder to see that Caro had moved from his booth and was now standing over the table where the Professor and his four young cohorts sat.

"Evening gentlemen," Caro said. "Sounds like a rather interesting conversation you're having."

"More to the point, it's a rather *private* conversation," Professor Novak responded curtly.

"Oh, come now, Professor. I'm sure there's room for one more in your little study group. After all, I think I know more about the Temple of Time than these four put together."

"I have no idea what you're talking about," Professor Novak said defensively.

"Do you think I'm stupid?" Caro asked with a laugh. "I've been studying the Temple of Time since I was a boy. What began as childhood intrigue has become my life's obsession. I've pored over maps, transcripts, books you probably don't even know exist."

"Caro, this topic in not open for discussion. Now if you'll excuse us, we must be leaving."

Max looked to see the four students each grab one of the items concealed in cloth. Professor Novak grabbed the book and shoved it into inside pocket of his jacket. He stood, but Caro blocked his way.

"Give me the book," Caro ordered, then turned to the others and demanded, "And I'll take the four pieces of the clock too if you don't mind."

"Or what?"

Caro pulled a switchblade knife, flicked the blade open and pressed it against the Professor's stomach. "Or your life's work ends here tonight."

The Professor didn't flinch at the touch of the blade resting against his gut. "Caro Sholtez, you're dabbling with powers you can't possibly comprehend."

"I know. And I'm tired of not comprehending them. I want to see them for myself. I want to see what it does. If the legend really is true, that is. There's only one way to find out. Now give me that book."

Suddenly Max stood from his booth and faced them all.

"Caro? Professor? What's going on?"

"Max?" the Professor asked. "What the hell are—"

But before he could finish his sentence, Lars stole his chance

The Tomb of Heaven

to grab the nearest pint glass on the table and splash the ale directly into Caro's eyes. Caro dropped the knife and stumbled backward, wincing and squinting and wiping frantically at his stinging eyes.

The Professor turned to his four students. "Run! Hide the pieces of the clock where nobody will ever find them! Guard them with your lives!"

The four nerds quickly slipped the cloth-covered items into their pockets and pushed their way across the floor of the crowded pub. Caro tried to grab Reynold's jacket. Professor Novak stopped him with a punch to the jaw, a blow that sent Caro reeling backwards into a group of drunken patrons.

"Hey!" one of the patrons shouted at Caro. "You wanna fight?"

He threw a swing at Caro but missed. Caro's fist however was on target, connecting with the drunken man's nose in a splash of blood. The man's friends lunged at Caro and he started fighting them off.

Max moved to help him, but Professor Novak grabbed Max by the shoulder. "Fathom, get out of here. Go home. Forget everything you heard. Forget that you were ever here."

"But Caro needs my help."

The Professor tightened his grip on Max. "I've never trusted that boy. You shouldn't either. If he knows as much as he says he does about the Temple of Time, then he can never get his hands on this book or the pieces of the clock. They're better off lost forever than in the possession of someone like Caro Sholtez."

"I don't know what you're talking about."

At that moment, the Professor looked over Max's shoulder to see Caro shoving the last of the drunkards off him and setting his sights on the Professor as more angry patrons began to charge toward him. Novak released Max's shoulder and turned to run. From behind, Caro barreled straight into Max.

"Get out of the way!" Caro shouted at him.

"Caro wait! What the bloody hell's going on?"

Someone swung a punch at Caro. He ducked and struck the man in the chin.

"It's none of your business so why don't you fuck off! You're a waste of my time, Fathom. You always have been!"

As if Caro's comment didn't hit him hard enough, a physical blow came from the left and struck Max square in the side of the face. He stumbled to his right before being caught by the lapels by another patron who shouted in his face, "That's my hat you're wearin'! Are you trying to steal my bloody hat?"

Max looked around, his vision a blur for a moment, trying to find Caro. But in the chaos of the bar brawl that was growing by the second, there was no sign of Caro to be seen. Max took the hat off his head, gave it to the angry gentleman and said, "My mistake," before staggering for the door, dodging more punches and drunken misaimed swings until he managed to push his way through the exit. He looked right and saw Ignatius, Reynold, Nicholas and Lars turn out of the cobblestone alley and vanish. He looked left and saw Caro sprinting as fast as he could after Professor Novak, the glowing face of Big Ben towering far above them in the background. It was almost midnight. Max poured on the speed, ignoring the Professor's advice to stay out of things as he chased after Caro.

Up ahead Max watched Novak turn left at the end of the alley, followed closely by Caro. With his shoes clattering against the cobblestone, Max almost slipped as he rounded the turn as fast as he could. Ahead he saw Novak racing towards Bridge Street, headed for Parliament Square. The headlights of passing vehicles lit up the street. Max could see Novak make a break for Bridge Street.

The Professor wasn't slowing down as he neared the road, and as Novak glanced over his shoulder to see Caro still in pursuit, he bolted headlong on to the busy street— directly in front of an

The Tomb of Heaven

oncoming double-decker bus. The horn blared. The bus braked. But it was too late.

With a loud thud, the bus knocked Professor Novak to the ground.

Caro pulled to a halt and froze.

Max stared in wide-eyed horror, rushing as fast as he could to the scene of the accident.

He slowed as he reached Caro and panted in panic, "What have you done?"

Caro said nothing, he did not move a muscle.

Max left him standing there and raced onto the street, kneeling beside Novak. "Professor! Professor, can you hear me?"

Novak was bleeding profusely from a head wound. He groaned and his eyes opened a fraction.

Behind Max, the stunned driver stepped out of the bus. "He came from nowhere! He didn't even look! What the bloody hell was he thinking?"

Max ignored the driver. He could feel tears of fear roll down his cheeks.

Novak's eyes focused on Max's. A smile spread across his face. "I knew you would find me, Max," he breathed, struggling to speak. "Someone told me a long, long time ago that you and I would find each other."

"Professor, stay calm. We'll get you help."

But Novak shook his head and reached into his jacket. Feebly, he dragged the book from his inside pocket. "The book. Take it, Max. Take it and run. Don't let Caro ever get his hands on it. Run, Max. Run!"

With that, Professor Novak sighed his last breath as his eyelids slid shut forever.

Max stared at him, overwhelmed with confusion and shock. He didn't know what to do. Bus passengers and passers-by were beginning to gather. Max shot a look through the crowd at Caro, who was staring straight back at Max. His eyes were cold. His face stony. And then Max saw it—Caro's gaze left Max's eyes and he glanced down at the book in Novak's dead fingers. Before Max knew what he was doing, he seized the book, jumped to his feet—and ran in the opposite direction of Caro.

From behind him the bus driver called out, "Hey, he just stole something!" But Max didn't stop. He didn't look back. He continued across Bridge Street, running as fast as he could in the beams of headlights, bringing traffic to a halt as horns sounded and cars swerved to miss him.

Only when he reached Parliament Square did he turn for a second to see Caro darting across the street after him. Max kept running, heading straight for the shadowy alcoves of the Palace of Westminster, desperate for a place to hide or a path that might throw Caro off his trail. He raced along the side of the building, past doorways and dark recesses, until suddenly someone grabbed him and pulled him into the shadows.

Max wanted to scream for help before a voice with a Norwegian accent whispered, "Max, it's me. Lars."

"The Professor's dead," Max blurted in a distraught tone.

Lars covered Max's mouth with his hand. "I know. I saw. But we'll all be dead if you don't give me that book."

Max resisted. "What's going on? Tell me what's happening."

Lars shook his head. "You're safer not knowing. Just give me the book. Then run. Run as fast as you can."

Max realized what Lars was suggesting. "You're going to use me as bait?"

"Caro will think you still have the book. It's the only way to keep the secret safe." Lars glanced across Parliament Square to see Caro approaching. "There's no time to argue. The book, Max. Give me the book, please."

Trusting his gut, Max shoved the book into Lars' hands. Instantly, Lars turned and vanished into the darkness. Max turned in the opposite direction, trying one door handle after another until one turned, unlocked. Max pushed his way through the door and into what looked like the corridor of an emergency exit, illuminated with bare bulbs and lined with pipes and plumbing.

The door behind him slammed shut. Max knew Caro would have heard the sound of it closing. Max hurried along the corridor, turned into a stairwell, then pushed his way through another door with a sign that read: *Elizabeth Tower Access*. Immediately he found himself at the foot of a staircase that wound all the way up the tower better known as—

"Big Ben," Max breathed. "I'm inside the tower of Big Ben."

Knowing there was a good chance Caro was in pursuit, Max had no choice but to climb. He took the steps three at a time, bounding his way upward, using the handrail to pull himself along as fast as he could. He was halfway up when he heard the door far below open and close. Max stopped climbing the stairs. He pulled away from the railing, backed himself up against the wall and froze.

"Max?" echoed Caro's voice up the tower. "I know you're in here. Why don't you come down and give me the book?"

Max did not respond.

Caro's voice called up to him again. "What are you going to do when you get to the top, Max? You wouldn't want to fall from way up there, would you?"

Max still did not speak. Caro remained silent, waiting for a response.

Seconds passed.

Max heard the door below open and close once more. He breathed a sigh of relief, realizing Caro had gone to look for him elsewhere.

Slowly, silently, Max stepped toward the handrail and peered over the edge, looking all the way down to the bottom of the stairwell... looking for any sign of Caro. For a moment he saw nothing.

Then suddenly— with a grin on his face, Caro appeared down

below, looking up and spotting Max instantly. "A-ha! Tricked you!" With that, Caro started storming up the steps.

In a heart-pounding panic, Max kept climbing, faster than before. His legs were burning and his feet began to slip on the stairs. Caro was stronger, more athletic than Max. He knew Caro would be gaining on him with every leap he took up the stairwell. Soon Max could see the top of the tower coming into view. He reached the last of the steps.

He raced through an open doorway, into a short steel staircase, and emerged on the upper deck of the tower. Enormous steel beams crisscrossed the space. To his left was a door labeled *Mechanism Room*, while above him hung the colossal bell of Big Ben, its mighty hammers resting against its curved side, while surrounding it hung the chime bells.

Max heard the pounding footsteps of Caro's feet as he reached the top of the steps. Quickly Max opened the door to the Mechanism Room. He was met with the buzz, whir and tick of dozens of cogs and gears of all sizes spinning in the center of the room. Some were the size of a dinner plate, others the size of a cart wheel. They turned and spun at different speeds, each cog connected to the next, keeping time in perfect balance. But not for long. Almost as soon as Max had closed the door behind him, Caro came bursting into the Mechanism Room.

"Looking for a place to hide?"

Max immediately began backing away. "Caro, I don't know what's going on here, but you're frightening me."

"You should be frightened. You've blundered into the middle of something much bigger than you'll ever understand, Max." He began to step menacingly towards Max, who took a step back for every step Caro took forward. "Didn't your mother tell you not to stick your nose into other people's business? Oh, that's right, you don't have a mother. She died. Perhaps it's one of those lessons you're going to have to learn the hard way. Now give me the book, Max."

The Tomb of Heaven

Max shook his head. "I don't have it."

He began to back his away around the cogs filling the center of the room, eyeing the door.

"I saw you take it from Novak's cold, dead hand," Caro said. "I know you have it. Now hand it over."

Max tried to make a break for the door, but Caro was quick and cut off his escape. He seized Max by both arms. "I'm not playing games here, Max."

"Neither am I. I don't have it."

Max tried to pull out of Caro's grip as the young man he had made love to only hours earlier tried to reach inside his jacket in search of the book. Max pushed him away, then stumbled precariously close to the whirring cogs.

Too close.

The end of Max's scarf got caught in the mechanism. Two cogs chewed up the end of the scarf and instantly pulled Max's head down toward the grinding wheels. Max pulled back hard, the scarf knotting tightly around his neck. It began to strangle him.

"Caro, help me," he choked.

But Caro was too busy pulling Max's jacket off his back, peeling it down his arms and searching through the pockets. "Where is it!" he shouted.

Max desperately tried to untie his scarf, pulling at the knot around his neck as the cogs pulled his face closer and closer to the churning gears. With only inches to spare, his fingers managed to slip the knot loose. The gears tried to devour his scarf, but it became caught in the sequence of cogs, jamming them. The mechanism groaned and smoke began to billow from it. Max staggered backward, gasping for air— and walked straight into Caro's bunched fist. As the blow slammed into Max's face, Max tried to stumble toward the door as smoke filled the room.

"Where's the book! Who has the book!" Caro screamed with rage.

Suddenly a loud series of cracks like gunshots filled the room as the teeth of several cogs broke off and shot through the air. One grazed Caro's cheek like a bullet, distracting him momentarily. Max made a bolt for the door. He grabbed the handle, yanked the door open and ran. Caro was only steps behind him.

As Max bolted down the steel steps toward the stairwell, he stole a glance back to the bell, its hammer now pulling away from the side of the bell, ready to sound midnight. The chime bells began to ring, although their tune seemed chaotic and crazed as smoke poured from the Mechanism Room.

The hammer teetered over Big Ben, ready to fall.

Max began to descend the stairwell, fleeing from Caro who was now right behind him. But Caro caught him by the collar of his shirt. He yanked hard and Max hit the handrail. He lost his balance. Then with one hard shove, Caro pushed Max over the railing. Max felt himself falling and grabbed the only thing he could— Caro's hand. Dangling over the handrail, gripping as tightly as he could to Caro, Max looked down and saw the drop below him plunging all the way to the bottom of the tower.

He looked up into Caro's eyes. "Pull me up! Caro, please!"

But Caro simply smiled the coldest, most sinister smile Max had ever seen.

The cacophony of the chime bells continued to ring through the tower.

Max pleaded. "Caro, I love you. I've always loved you."

Caro laughed, then sneered. "Don't waste my time. It's far too precious."

In the Mechanism Room, the cogs ripped the scarf to shreds. The gears spun faster than ever. And the hammer fell against the side of Big Ben.

The deafening toll of the giant bell sent a tremor down the clock tower—

—as Caro let go of Max's hand.

The fall should have killed him, but it didn't.

Max Fathom tried to clutch every railing his fingers could snatch on the way down as he tumbled through the air, plummeting down the length of the tower, his fingers grabbing and slipping, grabbing and slipping, until finally he hit the stone, cold floor at the bottom of the tower.

He spent the next six weeks in an induced coma. He spent another month in hospital recovering, his head and eyes wrapped in bandages.

He had been questioned by police countless times over the break-in at Big Ben and the death of Professor Novak, but no sense could be made of the incidents of that night. There was no longer any trace of the other students involved. Ignatius Swinborne, Nicholas Ayres, Reynold Rafferty, Lars Valhalla and Caro Sholtez had all simply vanished without a trace.

When Max's bandages were finally removed, his doctor asked him, "How do you feel?"

"I feel fine," he answered. "But when can you take the bandages off my eyes?"

There was a pause before his doctor answered, "We have."

Max shook his head. "But I can't see. I can't see anything."

ABOUT THE AUTHOR

Robin Knight is the author of gay fiction novels, novellas and short stories, ranging in genre from gay adventure, gay romance, gay suspense and gay comedies.

The heroes of Robin's books love to spend their time jumping off the page, stumbling through misadventures and falling in love.

Robin has worked in advertising, politics, journalism and event management, but nothing is as fun as telling stories.